ONCE I LIVED

'Once I Lived,

Natascha Wodin

Translated by Iain Galbraith

Library of Congress Catalog Card Number: 91-67838

British Library Cataloguing in Publication Data
    Once I Lived, – (Masks series)
    I. Title   II. Galbraith, Iain   III. Series
    823.914 (F)

    ISBN 1-85242-221-1

First published as *Einmal lebt ich* by
Luchterhand Literaturverlag GmbH, Frankfurt am Main, 1989,
© 1989 by Luchterhand Literaturverlag GmbH

Cover photograph of the author
copyright © Marianne Fleitmann

This translation copyright © 1992 by Serpent's Tail

This edition first published 1992 by
Serpent's Tail, 4 Blackstock Mews, London N4 and
401 West Broadway #2, New York, NY 10012

Typeset in 10½/13½pt Garamond by Contour Typesetters, Southall
Printed in Hungary by Egyetemi Nyomda, Budapest

I have studied the science of parting:
I studied it at night . . .

Osip Mandelstam

I border on a word still, and on a different country;
I border, not much perhaps, but more and more on all . . .

Ingeborg Bachmann

In memory of my mother

ONCE I LIVED

For a few days, I thought you were going to be the first person to belong to me, the first person not to regard me as undesirable, or with indifference, the first living being to need me. For a few days I loved you with all the love, all the affirmation my own life lacked. I thought of you as the first person who *had* to acknowledge my presence. You, a child, were everything to me that I, a child, could not live without: protection, refuge, support, shelter. You were everything I should have been to you. You were everything that felt jeopardized and vulnerable in me, everything whose protection and survival demanded all the strength that my own sense of menace and vulnerability could muster. I had always been lonely, as lonely as only a child can be. Now I had something nobody could take from me: you, my very own possession, my very own human being. I, a child, had a child. I no longer wished for a friend, no longer wished for a family, things that I had constantly envied others for as if they were the miracles of a normality from which I alone were excluded. I even stopped talking to my mother, the only person I felt acknowledged me and knew me. You weren't wishful thinking – like my friend. You weren't unattainable – like a family. You weren't dead – like my mother. You were inside me. You were growing: palpable, real, almost visible. You weren't a second, separate being who could leave me or turn your back to me at any moment. We were one flesh, one blood, one breath. For the first time in my life I was not alone.

But then – I was too alone with you. And you were too alone with me. A child, you were alone with a child who was alone with a child. You were the child of the man who had twice raped me, and so you couldn't be my child. You were a foreign body inside me, a body forced on me; *his* body, which had broken into me with brute force and grown in me ever since. You were not the thing that was jeopardized in me, the thing that needed my protection. You were the thing that was endangering me, the thing working against me, which I was supposed to bear, supposed to give birth to. I was your breeding place, and you were *his* body, which had struck root in me and was feeding on me through you, sucking out my lifeblood, lodged in me like a deadly growth. I was one flesh, one blood, one breath with *him*, the monster that thrived on me: palpable, real, almost visible. And I began to hate you. I began to kill you. Let me tell you the story of what happened before your time, the story of a short life in the world you never knew, and the story of your death – which only you know.

I am no expert – not even on the things I have loved most. These have stayed with me as scattered images and have nourished my life with memories and emotions, but they have done nothing to cultivate the desertlike state of my mind.

Natalia Ginzburg

My first worldly sounds: "Two little Italians", "La guitarra brasiliana" and "We're going out tonight" by Conny and Peter. On Wednesday evenings, when my father was out on the late shift, I would listen to Fred Rauch's radio request programme. Elvis Presley, the first warning notes of a storm called "The Beatles", the latest dances with names like "Twist" and "Rock'n' Roll" – all these I heard for the first time ... The girls in my new class wore petticoats and stiletto heels. They had high, back-combed hair and wore nail varnish. These were the years of the "economic miracle" in a German provincial backwater. But for me, this was the world itself. After five years of walls, classrooms, dormitories, rosaries, matins, complines, High Mass and spiritual exercises; after five years of rare glimpses of a town that looked like a huge, richly ornamented gravestone; after five years spent breathing the air of a debtors' prison where debts were never redeemed but grew and grew with every breath until eventually they suffocated you; after five years at convent school – this was freedom. Even life in the "houses" that I had now returned to was bliss by comparison, if only because I could leave them.

On the evenings when my father was on late shift, I would go out parading on the High Street. Oh, just to be there and be seen by other people! To catch a glimpse of others, of German girls, to see what they had on, how they moved, how they exchanged glances with the German boys! And to go window-shopping – nylon blouses, raglan pullovers, blue-jeans, tight "Trevira" skirts with slits, the first bikinis nobody dared wear! The High Street – that grand promenade, that central catwalk, the very hub of the world! And only one destination: marriage! To be German at long last! To escape from the terrible "houses", as the people in town called them, houses where the homeless lived, refugees from the East, houses that were anything but home . . . To throw aside those charity and American CARE-package clothes! To get outside my terrible Russian skin! I'd heard you could do it at sixteen – get married; and I was sixteen, and half a year over already.

"Just you get one 4 in your school report," my father had said to me, while I stood at the mirror, cutting my fringe above a forehead that was much too high, much too bare. The entire story of my childhood had been a history of my having to suffer people's amazed reactions at a "Russian forehead" I didn't want. "Just one 4," said my father, "and you'll be straight back in that convent." I'd rather have died than go back to that oubliette, those leaden chambers, where you fell and fell all day long, even in your sleep, as if weights were dragging you down in one long fall to hell. Only marriage could help me now. That 4 in my school report – I could feel it in my bones – was inevitable. I only had a few weeks left.

One day I made a discovery in the attic, a hemp sack containing clothes of my mother's that had gone missing, had simply vanished from our flat with as little warning as when she herself had disappeared. My father must have stuffed them in this sack and taken them up to the attic straight after her funeral, as if he had needed to bury my mother a second time, as if she weren't dead enough already, and as if he had thereby sealed a bond of eternal silence over my mother, a silence that lay over her like a second tombstone. Suddenly, there I was, holding them in my hands: her blue rayon dress with its white lace trimmings, her grey dress with peacock's eyes; all that semi-outdated American stuff, already half mouldy, sent – along with tinned cheese, Russian halva and colour photos of wooden, one-storey houses with cars parked in front of them – by people who had managed to escape our storeyard barracks for America. We had always gone around, out of time and place, in these clothes that were usually too big or too tight, looking like an outlandish, absurdly adorned group of scarecrows. And here was I holding that taffeta dress with its brightly coloured bunches of flowers and gathered lap, the dress in which I could picture her standing on the station platform, just as she had done six years earlier. I had come back from Petit Thier and nothing would "ever be the same again", as she had written on the Russian card she sent to the farm in Belgium where I had stayed for a year, almost happy for the first time in my life. Walking along beside her, beside this flowery dress with its gathered lap, it was as if my mother were no longer really there, had already stopped living, no longer spoke, no longer saw me. And then I was holding her grey coat with its velvet collar and cuffs, which they had found by the river, and in which I had seen my mother again and again at night, in dreams, coming home, turning the corner up by the bridge, where the road branched off from the High Street to the "houses". And suddenly I was holding the green pullover with grey diamonds on its breast in which I had last seen her, in which I had always imagined her, lying against the embankment where they had found her, half in the weeds, half in the water, near the big, flat stone where we used to go on summer evenings to fetch water for our allotments, and where, sometimes, in the heat of the summer, I had dived into the dark green flow, whose surface was quite smooth close to the bank but whose current was very strong, so that even then the cold, bottomless torrent had filled me with a strange sense of dread. And all those years, I had seen my mother lying there in that green pullover with its grey diamonds, with those very small, shrunken, woollen diamonds on her breast; and suddenly, I was holding the pullover in my hands. Suddenly, it was as if I had never known anything about my mother, as if everything else about her had disappeared along with my realisation that she must have changed her clothes again before she left, as if, once again, she were fading from sight along with the little grey diamonds which had vanished from her breast, with nothing but emptiness to replace them in my mind. And the pullover in my hands no longer seemed to be the first, visible evidence of my mother's existence; rather it showed that the mantle of silence spread over my mother by my father had in fact been the expression of my own, merely imaginary picture of her.

This hemp sack was where I found the two odd nylon stockings I wore when I went to the High Street in the evenings, the bra into which I had to stuff handkerchiefs because my breasts were too small, the mussel-coloured petticoat which I secretly starched with flour, the cherry-red, American high-heels I had to stuff with newspaper so they would fit me, and which I had to keep hidden from my father. I was forbidden anything red. According to my father, red was the colour of harlots. He never gave me any money, not even for things I really needed. I secretly cut up sheets and towels and stuffed them into my knickers once a month. "If I ever get wind that you've been hanging about in town, I'll kill you," he said. "My daughter's no whore!"

I'd been good at school in the convent. But here, in my new, worldly school, I had gone to the bottom of the class almost overnight. In the convent I'd been different, too, because I wasn't Catholic. I only knew the Russian way of crossing yourself, the Russian prayers and chants. I hadn't been allowed to go to confession like the others; I had to remain seated in the pew when the others took Communion. As a child, I hadn't had to wait for first Communion to be one of Christ's little white brides. I'd been held up to the Russian priest at the age of three, held up before the great beard of the Lord, before the great chalice of wine and *prosvirka*. When I'd first gone to the convent, I hadn't known that you weren't allowed to eat meat on Fridays, or that, when you were having a bath or using the toilet, you had to be quick about it, because to see youself like that was a sin. I hadn't known there were countless mortal sins, which, if you didn't confess them, sent you to hell. I was still different when the bishop allowed me to go to confession and take Communion like the others; because I still wasn't a Catholic, and not being Catholic was worse than not being German. Not to be German was to be damned in this life, but not to be Catholic was to be damned for Eternity. And my father would never have allowed me to become a Catholic. I stayed Russian Orthodox. Confession and Communion, morning mass in the convent chapel, prayers to Our Lady in the church of St. James, Sunday Mass in the cathedral, and every single day at the convent itself were all merely favours for which I had to be grateful.

But now, in my new school, being Catholic was no longer important. In fact it was wrong, since everybody here was Protestant, which I couldn't become either. But worst of all, I was the "Russki" from the "houses" all over again, just as I had been as a child – a leper nobody talked to. The character of my abnormality seemed to change like the colours of a chameleon, even though outwardly, I was the greyest, most nondescript of them all. Possibly only comparable, I supposed, with Inge Krabbe. Inge Krabbe came from the houses near the "houses", from the last German houses before you came to the plot of land that had been set aside for us, on which no German had probably ever set foot, unless you included policemen or other public officials. Not even Inge Krabbe, that most miserable of Germans, would speak to me, and usually I couldn't understand what people at school were saying anyway. My lack of German was even more obvious in this new and perplexing world than it had been at the convent. There, the fear of God had lain like a veil over all things real. Even in geography, mathematics and chemistry, we were judged more for our piety than for knowledge of such earthly things, in which lurked evil and sin; my good marks at the convent had been more a reward for santimoniousness than for knowledge or diligence. Suddenly, I was having to deal with naked, unexpurgated mathematics, naked geography and chemistry. I hadn't known there was such a thing, and saw at last what the convent had kept hidden. Suddenly it was as if there were two German languages – a Catholic one, and a new, alien one that belonged to a baffling world where everyone was way ahead of me, and even fractions and dates in history meant something different than they had at the convent, where the words in the novels and newspaper articles they used in German and social studies lessons had almost no meaning for me whatsoever. The only German books I had held in my hand previously were the school textbooks and prayer-books we'd been allowed at the convent, and the only other books I knew were the volumes of Russian poetry and fairytales of my childhood – plus the

Russian émigré newspapers my father subscribed to. But while my poor German hadn't been noticed at the convent, or, at least, had been overshadowed by the far graver fault of my not being Catholic, now my foreignness seemed to erupt from me whenever and wherever the chance arose, like the symptoms of some rare disease or mutation. I couldn't understand the language the teachers spoke, the language the pupils spoke, the language of the boys whom I suddenly found sitting beside me in class, the language the boys spoke to each other, the language of the girls to each other, the language spoken between boys and girls, between pupils and teachers, who now addressed us in the polite "Sie" form, and said "Fräulein" to me. Suddenly, I had become a grown-up; people were saying "Sie" to me. But it seemed to me that it was only what was Russian and shameful in me that had grown up, whereas the hope of growing into a German – my lifelong desire, whose fulfilment would mark the true beginning of life for me – dwindled as I sat (stuttering and blushing) on the school bench, shrank with every question I was asked and couldn't understand, even though I jumped up from my seat whenever my name was called out just as we'd been taught at convent. A surge of derisive laughter would force me back down onto the bench, and a 4 in my report, a verdict of "unsatisfactory" in every subject, being sent back to convent – it all seemed increasingly inevitable. I sat on my bench just as I had at morning mass in the convent chapel, during prayers to Our Lady in St. James's, or at Sunday Mass in the cathedral, and something dreadful kept pressing to get out of me. There was some uncontrollable part of me that led a life of its own. At convent it had been my laughter, a laughter without any reason at all. I had been powerless against it. It had brewed somewhere inside me, come gurgling up my throat in bubbles and, as if its aim were to unmask some devastating truth about myself of which I knew nothing, it had threatened to burst out at precisely those moments when I was required to show the greatest seriousness and most solemn devotion. This irrepressible truth now resided in my bladder, a constant reminder of the most mortifying experience of my life, which happened when I was seven or eight. My mother had given me money and sent me on my first ever visit to the hairdresser's. Somewhere between trepidation and ecstasy, placed upon a genuine hairdresser's chair, a bit like chairs I had seen at the dentist's, and intoxicated by perfumes and by all the luxury around me, I had sat in impatient anticipation of my metamorphosis from an ugly duckling with ruffled plumage to a lovely German princess with bobbed hair. But suddenly, right in the middle of this transformation, I noticed a peculiar change come over the face of the hairdresser in the big round mirror in front of me. She had interrupted her cutting quite abruptly, and now disappeared behind a curtain, from which, a moment later, she reappeared, accompanied by a second hairdresser who proceeded to bend back my ears, looking first behind the left, then the right. And then I heard the word "lice". And as if that were not enough, as if, though already red-hot with shame, I needed fully to plunge into the burning flames of ignominy, my bladder failed me. A warm wetness began to seep down my stockings and drip to the floor, across which were swarming the lice that had crawled from the snippets of my hair. A whole army of them, soaked in my urine that had seeped through onto the hairdresser's chair and was now forming puddles on the delicate blue linoleum, wreaked their havoc upon the hair of the German ladies. The last thing I knew was that the hairdresser's cape was taken off me, and then – nothing. It was as if my humiliation had finally, and mercifully, reduced me and all my dire affliction to ashes. Only out on the street did I come to myself, a cold, sticky wetness on my head and legs, as I made my long way back through town, crowned with half a German pageboy cut – upon which crawled my Russian lice.

A disgrace of similar proportions now seemed set to break over me as I sat on the school bench, the perfidious liquid gradually collecting in my pelvis just as the laughter once had in my throat. Already, I sensed those minute vibrations in the air that announced the guffaws of my fellow pupils whenever I had to leap up for the second or third time between breaks and rush to the toilet – always waiting until the very last moment before the dam burst with such a force that it took all the strength of my sphincter to withstand it. Again and again, I had to run the gauntlet of my fellow pupils' mockery as I fled to the toilets, the gauntlet of my own pathetic catastrophe. It was always the same. What people saw in me was always what made me so different from them. They always saw the opposite of something that had been invisible in me for such a long time now, and which I so urgently needed them to see. I needed them to see that I was the same as everyone else, that I belonged, that I was German and grown up, and that I was worthy of love.

The "houses" consisted of four long, flat-roofed constructions, painted white and containing a number of one-and two-room flats. Seven years after the end of the war, they had become the end of the line for a bunch of refugees from the East: Romanians, Bulgarians, Latvians, Lithuanians, Russians, Serbs, Croats, Hungarians, Poles, Czechs, Slovaks, Armenians, Georgians, Christians and Muslims. They were a motley crew who had had their fair share of transit camps and makeshift settlements, and now formed the melting-pot of a new nation: the nation of homeless, stateless and nameless persons. The "houses" surrounded a large courtyard with a German lawn, over which a German caretaker cast a suspicious eye. Two feeble birches swayed in the wind – a German building society's concession to the East. These were the very outskirts of the town, just before the fields and forests, the gravel-pits and riverside meadows began. Beyond here, beyond our own forlorn outpost, there were only the huts of the gypsies. This was my big adventure playground, the free-ranging wilderness of my childhood. Our windows and doors were always left open, lending the yard the air of a Balkan village. At the same time, this was perhaps the only thing that distinguished the "houses" from a prison, their only semblance of freedom – and it was exploited to the full in all weathers. Here was the Babylon of the East, where the dregs of many languages had jelled into a single, common language: the Esperanto of the scum. They were *our* houses, our own world, separate from the world of the Germans.

I still think of Marjanka, the Polish woman who lived next door to us, fat Marjanka with the watery eyes, whose contourless body always seemed to be finding its way into the hands of men. For a while she had lived nowhere and everywhere, anywhere she could find a bed for the night. Then she would get pregnant, be beaten up, and be chucked out on the street again. Eventually, our neighbour, a Romanian with a wooden leg, took her in, his deeply choleric distrust preventing her from venturing astray again. He beat her and made her pregnant, just like the others. He fed all her nameless Eastern offspring, and tetchily defended his honour in the yard. But Marjanka didn't live long. For a while, she managed to drag herself about in the yard on her dropsied legs, and then, one day, she simply lay down and didn't get up. The stench of rotting nappies and alcohol steamed over from her flat. Her children blubbered apathetically. Scabby with dirt, they sat on the windowsill overlooking the yard, death already writ large in their faces, clinging together like mangy little animals.

I still think of the Serbian family who lived above us, the wife whose black, speechless eyes alone were visible through a jumble of veils. And in those eyes I could see the screams which I heard above us every Saturday when the men drank away their welfare money or week's wages. They were like the piercing yelps of an animal, screams of mortal terror, mixed with the furious howls of the husband and the crashing and splintering of furniture. And then, in the utmost depths of her distress, when no one seemed to hear her cries, the woman started to scream for help in German. Perhaps "help" was the only German word she knew, the only German word that had any meaning for her, but her screams of terror were as much in vain in German as in Serbian.

I think of the old, Latvian couple whom we thought of as "refined". I see the dark square of an open window, through which you could hear the clattering of a typewriter, occasionally interrupted by the dull chime of a clock. I sat there once as a child and was given my first ever liqueur to drink. I sat in their gloomy flat, lined with Russian books and framed photographs, and their clock seemed to strike a different time, a time that was null and void. And we would see the old Latvian sitting at his window, day after day, year after year, statuesque, a mighty Baltic skull weathering in a window frame . . .

I think of Farida, my secret friend, who was forbidden to talk to me because I had seduced her into adventurous expeditions to the German town, into stealing apples and plums, into playing by the gravelpits and in the meadows until late on summer evenings, and into showing each other what was under our skirts. Later, when I came back from the convent, her problems were more or less the same as mine: she was only allowed to leave the "houses" when she went to school; she wasn't allowed to talk to German boys; she was beaten up by her Muslim father and locked in her room. Her fear of her father made it impossible for her to speak to me any longer. After all, I was the girl who paraded up and down the German High Street in red high-heels when her father was on late shift.

I think of the terrifying giant – I have no idea where he came from – who had the shoulders of a mammoth and the arms of a gorilla. He had chased his German wife away and had taken a gypsy woman from the huts down by the gravel-pits – the gypsy huts, which even we thought of as places of ill repute. She was tiny, like a gnome, and she would walk beside this giant across our yard, neither of them saying a word. They never spoke, probably because neither one understood the language of the other, and because they never had anything to say to each other anyway. And she always wore the giant's grey jacket, which, on her, reached almost to the ground. Perhaps she was hiding behind it the gypsy she still was: black-haired, dark-skinned, jangling with jewellery, the hem of her skirt gathered in a row of black rose-petals. And thus, at the side of her giant, she would pass through our yard, a survivor of the German gas-chambers.

I think of the old, pale-faced Russian hunchback who would come flailing his arms and legs through our yard, preaching that our end was nigh, and who would wave a copy of *Watchtower* in his hand, attempting to convert us, who were homeless in this life, to the coming kingdom of Jehovah.

I think of the young newly-wed Czech with the sticking-plaster over one eye who played the concertina in the yard. He would sit outside his door and play for hours and days on end. He would play on and on with a rollicking, obsessive jollity, and I was always worried my mother would close the window and break down sobbing: "I can't go on – I can't bear it any more – I'll go mad." And one day the Czech was found in his flat, lying on the floor in the blood on which he had choked to death as it burst from his tattered lungs.

I think of the much-thumbed, black-and-white photo of a small Armenian boy in a German sailor suit who had become what I so passionately wanted to be, the adopted child of German parents. It had an almost legendary aura for me, that photo. Time and time again, the bald Armenian with gold fillings would take it out of his jacket pocket, his eyes full of tears, cursing himself in his Armenian-Russian-German gibberish. And I see his petite young wife, her body exhausted with pregnancy, whose job was to give the Armenian back his lost son, but who gave birth only to daughters, one every year, a whole bevy of little girls with black eyes and black curly hair, done up like little princesses, all playing in the yard instead of his son.

I think of the Bulgarian whose wife fell over while ironing and died of an intestinal blockage. Marjanka lived with him for a while. Then there was a third woman, and a fourth. I' remember the inexplicable fear that gripped me whenever I came near this man in his fine grey suit, his creepy looks that seemed to lurk in the yard, ready to ambush me, encircle me, like a spider weaving its greedy, deadly web around me. Only a miracle helped me escape the sinister intentions that lay behind those looks. The Bulgarian was supposed to be driving me to a German orphanage after the death of my mother, and my father – miracle of miracles – suddenly decided he was going to come along after all . . . After five years away from the "houses", I returned to find the Bulgarian at death's door. The very figure of death, he hobbled through the yard on crutches, was collected by ambulance twice a week for blood treatment, and one day didn't come back.

I think of the first Germans who came to live in the "houses" at the beginning of the sixties. Now *they* were the ostracised minority, the enemy; *they* were invaders who had no right to occupy our territory, our bit of land, the only prerogative we had.

Living above us was a woman with a massive, hippo- potamus-like body, gaps in her front teeth and shiny, black, bobbed hair. It was said she'd been caught in a shop stealing coffee and schnaps, and that she had lovers and regularly beat up her husband. The latter was a spindly, jaundiced little creature whose lung disease had forced him into early retirement. He would sit outside the flats with a bottle of beer in his hand, warming his wasted limbs in the sun. And on winter's days, you'd see a dirty little girl with a scrawny neck and tousled, curly hair, pulling a battered handcart across the yard with a small pile of coal on it. Almost every day, the same, pathetic little demonstration of poverty; this seven- or eight-year-old whom you never saw playing, who didn't even seem to go to school, who did the housework, and kept her mother's lovers in beer and schnaps. You'd hear them beating her behind closed doors; and always the same sight, ill from the hidings she'd taken, sick with exhaustion, dragging just enough coal for a day on that miserable handcart through the yard.

I think of the German twins, two young men with sandy crew cuts. Distant and withdrawn, they'd come across the yard in their white, painter's overalls, each the double of the other, inseparable. Or you'd see them after work in their hound's-tooth check jackets, pushing their disabled father – a one-legged, paralysed war veteran – through the yard on a wheel-chair.

I think of shy Wilfried with his golden locks, the son of a German war widow, whom I fell in love with when I was little. Once we we were hiding in the cellar and I felt his big dry lips touch me in the dark. I was scared and ran away. But later, when I was at the convent, I thought of him as the only person outside who still knew me, and who was perhaps even waiting for me. But he was gone when I came back to the "houses". For love of another, a German girl, he had thrown himself under a train at the age of nineteen.

And I think of the young, black-haired Ukrainian woman, the sick eyes in her tortured face, and how, in the year Soviet tanks rolled into Hungary, in the year the Federal Republic of Germany once again armed itself against the enemy in the East, she had sunk into stony silence, and, in the thirteenth year of her life as a refugee in Germany, had drowned herself in the river – my mother.

On Saturday evenings, when the yard was surging like a huge living room full of babbling people, my father would heat the stove for his bathwater. There was nothing more excruciating to me than weekends with my father, when I had to do the housework as well as my homework. From Saturday when school was over until Monday morning when I went back to school, I was not allowed out of the flat and was nothing but my father's maidservant. I only escaped this prison during the weeks my father was on late shift from three until midnight. When he was on early shift, he would watch over me all afternoon and evening. But even then, I had a couple of hours freedom between leaving the prison that was school and returning to the prison that was our flat. Until he came home in the afternoon, I could at least wander about in town. I would hang about on the High Street, or in the dark alleys between the half-timbered houses down by the old millstream – it didn't matter where, as long as I didn't have to go back to the "houses".

The weekends, rather than being something to look forward to, became an even worse imprisonment than the convent. There, at least, you could spend what little free time you had out in the garden, or in the courtyard. For a short while at least you could escape Sister M.'s omnipresent gaze. But whenever my father was at home, I wasn't even allowed to set foot outside the door. The weeks my father was on late shift were my only rays of hope. Without them, I should never have been able to get through those desolate weeks when he was on early shift and I was his slave, or those utterly unbearable weekends.

I led a double life, of which my father suspected nothing, Or maybe it was because he did suspect me, perhaps it was because he knew I spent the hours he wasn't there on the German High Street in my red high-heeled shoes, that he never left the flat except for work. Even in the "houses", we didn't belong. My father never went out into the yard, never spoke to anyone. When he came home from work, he just sat down at the kitchen table and read and smoked. He sat, read and drank red wine, sat and read his Russian émigré newspapers, read Russian books that were sent to him from a Russian émigré library twice a month. For as long as I could remember, he had always been one of the reading dead, an inhabitant of some Russian world beyond our own, a stone sphinx. He was my prison guard who read and read. At the "houses", he commanded a certain respect. He was seen as an artist, a man of the world. Before becoming a factory worker, he had travelled the world with a Russian émigré choir. His voice had been heard on the radio and pictures of him in traditional Cossack dress admired on posters. Between tours he had come home wearing fine suits and bearing exotic presents from distant lands. And even now, though his fame had waned, and although he had become a normal, unskilled worker just like most men at the "houses", he still had the air of a fine, rather reserved gentleman surrounded by riffraff, a highbrow, who had given his daughter a proper education. And since he was also the widower of a woman who had committed suicide, he was shrouded in a tragic mystery that nobody dared penetrate. Nobody rang at our door. No one came to visit us as they had when my mother was alive. My father had neither friends nor enemies. He was a stranger amidst strangers, and nobody, least of all I, had any notion of what went on in his head. It would never have occurred to me that there *was* anything going on in that head. He was an inscrutable, reading sphinx, an unpredictable machine, whose iron parts would suddenly, with no warning at all, hit out at me.

My father usually beat me when my housework wasn't up to scratch. Even as a child I had lived in constant terror of his obsession with cleanliness and order. Nothing was ever clean enough or tidy enough; there was nothing my mother or I could do to satisfy him. We were incapable of attaining the standards set by the imaginary German housewives with whom he would continually compare us. Every speck of dirt we missed sent him flying into a rage. He called my mother a spoilt, slovenly good-for-nothing, who was careless with money, who couldn't cook, couldn't keep house, didn't know how to iron a shirt or sew buttons on properly. Why couldn't she be like the German housewives who knew how to handle money and whose houses were all spick and span? And eventually he would get onto the subject of my mother's family, her family genes, her Italian mother who'd been mad and had passed on her mental disease to my mother. And since I was so much more the daughter of my mother than of my father, I also became part of this Italian mental disease. In fact, there was nothing at all Italian about me. Outwardly, I was nothing like my mother. I had nothing of her thick, jet-black hair, or the sickly white delicacy of her fingers or her surprisingly large blue eyes; nothing of what made people call her an unusually beautiful woman, an unusually beautiful and unusually unhappy woman with whom I was only vaguely, inwardly, related – bonded in the depths of our common despair. In outward appearance, I was her opposite. I had thin, colourless hair. I was big-boned and broad-faced, and my features were typically Slavic. And these Slavic looks of mine even distinguished me from my gaunt-faced father, who also had black hair, so that I often imagined I was not really my parents' child at all. My mother nourished this belief in me, telling me the story of a foundling she had discovered in a ditch by the side of the road when she was fleeing from the East. She told me how my real mother had been blonde like me, a beautiful German woman who was rich and far away, and much nicer than my false, sickly mother, who was unhappy and homesick and full of bad luck. I was always overcome by a terrible need to weep whenever she told me this story in which I had two mothers and therefore none, in which I was at last the German child I had always wanted to be more than anything else in the world, but in which my German mother was beyond reach, so that I had only a Ukrainian-Italian mother to whom I was bound in indissoluble misfortune, in the calamity of our common oppression and hopelessness, abandoned to the pariah existence of our shared mental illness. But although I was supposed to have inherited this mental disease from my mother, to me it became a Russian disease, since it was the Russian in me that separated me from the Germans and made me inferior and abnormal in their eyes. Russianness was a disease of the mind *and* the body, and the older I got, the more bodily the disease became. The more, too, it became the disease of what was female in me, an irredeemable sin which, in me, was also something Russian.

Now that I was doing the housework instead of my mother, there was nothing I could do right. Saturdays were dreadful days of cleaning, and the more I scrubbed, scoured, wiped and polished, the more dirt my father seemed to find on the floor and doors and on the junk we called furniture. Now *I* was the one who was incapable of matching the standards of those imaginary German housewives. I wasn't allowed to do anything the German girls did. I wasn't allowed to go to the cinema, or to go dancing. I got no pocket money and was forbidden to buy nylons, never mind a petticoat or blue-jeans. And yet, I was still expected to be like a German girl, to be like one of those German housewives whose immaculate houses I had never set eyes on. When my father had inspected the floors, cupboards, doors and washbasins, he'd make me clean them again. I had to clean everything twice, or even three times, and because it still wasn't clean enough, he'd hit me. It was as if I myself were the dirt that I couldn't get rid of, and as if he had finally decided to wipe that dirt off the face of the earth with his own hands. I froze under his blows. In order to make myself harder than his fists, I imagined I was made of iron. It was the only way to stop him smashing me to bits. The only protection I had were the arms I held over my head while the barrage rained down on me.

Towards evening, my father would light the stove for his bath. On the window sill in the kitchen was a pan of red wine, which he warmed with a heating rod. He drank on other days, too, but on Saturday – cleaning and bathday – it was an absolute law. There was something different about his drinking on Saturdays, as if there were some strange and inexplicable correspondence between his drinking and the preparations for his bath. My father looked at me differently, too. It was no longer the hardness of his fists I felt on me, but something soft and moist and inquiring that rubbed against me and slithered about my legs and hips. And there was something in his look that stuck indelibly, like the dirt he found in the flat after I had cleaned it, something that even his fists couldn't erase, which had now merged with the dirt and sinfulness of the female body that I could no longer hide. His eyes fingered this dirt in me, as if trying to penetrate its deeper, resistant layers, and even the bath that he was about to take seemed linked to these endeavours. I had vague memories of times when I had sat on my father's lap of a Sunday, me in a baggy American Perlon dress, with the squiggly curls my mother had put into my hair. I'd spent a sleepless night lying on the metal curlers, dreaming of the gorgeous princess I'd be the following morning, and then there I was, all curls and Perlon, sitting on my father's lap. And just where his shirt opened, there was a pink little ball that grew out from his chest like a funny berry, and when I touched it my father snapped at my fingers with his teeth and puffed a swarm of hot little locusts through the Perlon onto my chest and tummy, until I almost couldn't breathe for laughing at the wonderful thrill of it. And when my father took my foot in his hand and pointed at my white shoe and asked me what it was, I knew what he wanted me to say, and so instead of saying "dyni", I said "pyni", and then he'd blow the little locusts under my white stocking.

I couldn't remember when these innocent games between my father and myself had come to an end, or when he had turned into the strange, threatening man he now was. Had it all started before my mother's death? Or was it only since I had come back to live alone with him after my five years of exile in which I had almost forgotten I had a father? One day, I had found myself in this unbelievable café, with mountains of red velvet plush and twinkling crystal lamps, and this unbelievable piece of chocolate cake on a plate in front of me, and sittng opposite me was a strange man in an elegant suit, a gold cigarette holder between his fingers, his face tanned by the sun of some country on a picture postcard – and it was my father. Suddenly he couldn't sing any more. His voice had cracked somewhere between the heat of a Spanish summer and a glass of cold wine which he had drunk too quickly.

Those precious vocal chords, which I had inherited, had won me the admiration of my German schoolmates as a child. They had allowed me the brief ecstasy of having my talents recognised at long last, though the exhilaration had never survived the next day at school, and from its heights I had always plunged into even greater depths of mockery and disdain. This voice of my father's no longer existed. There was just this silent, elegant man, whose broken voice had become my ticket back into the world.

It was time for my father to light the stove for his bath. First he scraped out the ash with the coalrake. This took some time, for he was slow and pedantic about it. He didn't send me down to the cellar, but went for the coal and wood himself, banging the bucket against the doorframe on his way back up, swaying with the effect of the red wine he had been drinking all afternoon. He would then demand that I watch while he demonstrated the correct procedure for lighting a fire, even though lighting the fire was a chore I dealt with every morning as a matter of routine. It was simply part of his Saturday bath ritual that he should light the stove himself, and that I should watch. Then, flushed from the hot red wine and from carrying the coal, he would take off his shirt. I saw the little pink lump protruding from above his white vest, the little bud of proud flesh with which I had played so blissfully as a child; and my sense of dread grew with every task I saw my father perform, as though I were being asked to learn something that would be of service to me at my own execution. I saw him spit into his hands and tear pages from a newspaper which he had taken from the pile under the sink. He then proceeded to crumple into balls the brownish pieces of paper with their Cyrillic print and vitriolic, medicinal smell, and to poke them into the stove, all the while taking the utmost care not to dirty his hands, and at the same time making it appear as if he were touching something holy, like a tabernacle. I saw him place the logs one by one on top of the paper, artistically arranging them in layers to achieve the secret geometry of maximum inflammability. I saw him take from his trouser pocket the petrol-lighter with its mysterious flints which I'd seen him use ever since my childhood, and apply the flame that danced up above his thumb to the paper. He would constantly interrupt these activities and reach for the large, white porcelain cup of warm red wine which stood beside him on the edge of the bath. He drank with his eyes half-closed, swaying with a barely discernible motion on his stool in front of the stove. He drank with the same expression of pleasure, the same almost ecstatic concentration on his face that he had while lighting the fire. And he would talk to himself continually, or to the things he was using. It was a confused, incomprehensible jumble of words that came out, but it always sounded as if he were goading things on, or praising them for obeying his hands.

When at last the fire was ablaze, he would close the stove door with a murmur of approval and wash his hands at the sink. And even doing this, he seemed to be demonstrating some procedure that would forever elude me and all my aspirations to the legendary cleanliness of the German housewife, washing dirt that was only invisible to me off hands which he had even managed to keep clean while lighting the fire. He lathered himself several times, right up to the elbows, and I saw the play of muscles on his naked arms, the twitching of small, unpredictable beasts under his yellow skin. I remembered then how he had taken me swimming in the river. It had been before we came to live near the river, when we had lived in a shed in the factory yard. He had lifted me onto the saddle of his bicycle and taken me somewhere where it was still and green, where the river was silent and dark and dreadful. But he took me in his arms and carried me into the water. Deeper and deeper he went, until he was wading up to his shoulders; and then he plunged me into the cold current and told me to swim. I screamed in fright. I had never been exposed to open water like this before, but my father's arms gripped me and held me down in the water, which immediately entered my lungs through my nose and mouth. Terrified, I tried to cling to my father's body. It was the only thing there was, the only possible salvation from this torrent that had no substance. But the only hope of rescue was also the very thing holding me under with its merciless pincers, wanting me to do something I couldn't do. And then suddenly it was all over. Suddenly a big green silence had enveloped me, a luminous green that rang in my ears, and I was drifting along in a cool, ringing light that held me and soothed me, and I wasn't even afraid of the wolves that my mother said lived on the bed of the river: "Let them eat me if they want to!" I thought, for I was part of that wonderful weightless ringing.

Then my father's face was there again through the explosion of sparks and glass splinters in my eyes, and everything inside me was scorching and burning and coughing, shaking me, tearing me more and more violently – away from the painless green ringing that had become me; and I would rather have died, because now I knew that dying was so light and lovely. But then my father's hands were twisting and pushing me again, back onto the saddle of the bicycle, back to the pain and fire which consumed my whole body.

Whenever my father went bathing in the open air he would have one of his attacks of malaria. He had brought this illness with him from some Asian part of the Soviet Union, from the Caucasus, where he had once lived. My picture of this other

Russian, Ukrainian, Asian, Caucasian part of my parents' lives was very vague. It was like my picture of the dinosaurs, or Neanderthal man in the Ice Age.

Confined to his bed, my father would be visited by dangerous and, to me, highly mysterious attacks of fever. I watched as he lay shivering and tossing on his bed with his stone-grey face and blue lips. His body, wrapped around with every available blanket, would tremble and quake for minutes at a time, as if at the mercy of some furious machine. My father's whole body seemed constructed from pieces of metal and glass whose thousand joints, like his chattering teeth, were banging against one another. After a while, in which his temperature had climbed to dizzy heights, he would break out in a sweat that released him from the fever's grip, and his temperature would drop as steeply as it had previously risen. The contraption of glass and metal would then change back into a living body. Under streams of sweat, my father's familiar face would emerge against his sodden pillow. His sheets, which my mother changed at regular intervals, would be collected in a sodden heap beside the bed, and my father would fall into an exhausted sleep. Several hours later, he would wake up freezing and shivering, and it would start all over again, the whole thing repeating itself a dozen times in the course of the next few days. But the strangest thing about this Asiatic disease called malaria was the medicine my father had to take for it: a floury, greenish-yellow powder that was kept in a tin right at the back of a cupboard and was called quinine. It was so bitter that its smell alone was enough to give me a bilious choking feeling. Horrified, I watched my father insert a whole tablespoon of the stuff between his teeth, which chattered and banged against the metal spoon as he did so, while my mother, her features distorted into a mask of revulsion, held a large glass of water ready. Struggling against the invisible machine that was shaking him, my father would guide the glass, his trembling hand spilling half its contents in the process, to his helplessly clattering jaws.

Malaria was the only illness my father had ever had. It was as if this illness itself were the source of his iron constitution. Or was it the quinine – the Asiatic antidote to his illness, the source of his bitter-smelling sweat and greenish-yellow, Asiatic skin – which brought on the malaria so regularly? My father's essence seemed to me to have mingled with that of the quinine; the dark powers of the Asiatic medicine were what gave his muscles their elasticity, and what made his fist so hard.

Every Saturday, while waiting for his bathwater to heat up, my father would sit at the kitchen table and clean his cigarette holder with a piece of wire and several, painstakingly rolled bits of newspaper. He was hot with the red wine and the work of lighting the stove, and with only a vest covering his torso, half his semi-naked body seemed the source of the heavy stench which now filled the whole flat. I saw him take the piece of wire and extract lumps of thick, black tar from within the golden shaft of his cigarette holder. It was like some disgusting substance that had come out of my father himself, and yet it was also the dirt which my father's eyes repeatedly sought in me, as if my body were full of nooks and crannies where this lascivious and yet utterly ineradicable dirt had collected. And the more the room and his eyes fogged up, the closer he seemed to his goal. There was no real reason for the dismay that I felt as I watched him clean this cigarette holder. There was only the way he looked at me. And yet I should not have been able to explain why his way of looking at me made me feel as I did – had there been anybody to explain it to. The only thing I could have said was that the key disappeared from the bathroom door one day, so that I had to get undressed and have baths behind a door that couldn't be locked. I could perhaps have added that when I was standing at the bathroom door with my nightdress and fresh towels over my arm, about to take my bath as usual before my father had his, I had suddenly heard him behind me asking whether he should wash my back. But how could I have explained my rigid terror, or the strange, helpless yap that had come out of my mouth when I said "no", like a little dog barking at a hyena that was about to deliver its final, deadly blow? In fact, that moment had given me a brief glimpse of *myself* as a murderer, and of my father crumpling under the blows of the iron poker that I brought crashing down on his head. These were the things that I couldn't explain, and which made *me* guilty and not him. Neither the disappearance of the bathroom key nor my father's offering to wash my back were proof of anything at all; the only proof was my own fear, and that was enough to fill me with guilt. So there I stood, paralysed with guilt, outside the white door which I had scoured three times and whose hidden dirt I alone failed to see.

The danger seemed to evaporate in the bathroom in a warm cloud of steam. I was alone, alone with myself in a world that dissolved into the cosy warmth that surrounded me and took on the phosphorescent colours of my dreams. Maybe I was far away somewhere, in America maybe, where girls like me got married to millionaires, or became famous filmstars overnight with the world at their feet. I lived in a villa with emerald palm trees bordering a blue swimming pool, and was picked up every evening by one of my admirers in a shining Cadillac. Or else I was married to a German craftsman. I lived with him in one of the fine German houses on Park Street – the perfect German housewife. My husband was very different from my father. He tipped his hat when he greeted people on the street, and he was never too embarrassed to know what to say when someone from the municipal authorities asked him something. My children were smart, well-mannered German girls with blonde curls; and they wore the nicest clothes and had the best marks in the school. I cooked German *sauerkraut* and German marinated beef, and on Sunday afternoon I had other German housewives round for coffee and cakes. I didn't know what I wanted to be more, an American filmstar or a German housewife. Both seemed equally distant, but I never doubted for a moment that one of the two would be my future. I sang softly to myself: "Two little Italians" . . . "Evening peace is all around us" . . . "Great Lord, we praise thee" . . . "*Golubym twoim sharfom igraya*" – I started. A noise. I got out of the bath as quickly as I could, and it wasn't until I felt the protective skin of the nightdress over me that my heart gradually stopped banging in my ears. A sick feeling in my stomach, I leant over the bath and began to clean it with scouring powder and a cloth. I felt I was trying to rub away my own body, but no matter how much I rubbed and scoured, that invisible, indestructible layer remained. It was the layer which, no matter how I rubbed and scoured, my father always discovered beneath the layer of dirt I cleaned, a layer of myself – ineradicable. Helpless, I left it to my father.

Flitting across the dark corridor, I sought the shelter of my bed. Presently, I heard footsteps outside the door. He staggered past, already very drunk. I heard the dull thud of his body against the wall, then, a scraping noise as his hand fumbled and pushed down the bathroom door handle. I didn't dare sleep. Petrified, I strained my ears to catch every sound – the water gushing out of the tap, the clatter of the poker, long silences in which there was only an occasional gurgling or splashing, and in which I thought I could hear my father's heavy wheezing. The only thing I really knew was that he always took the pan of hot red wine with him to the bathroom. But what he was doing there all that time I couldn't imagine. He would be there for two hours, or even longer, and these two hours seemed to be the climax of all his dealings with dirt. The sound of gushing water came again and again, grew in my ears to a roaring, surging orchestra through the wall. My nose filled with the steamy smell of soap and red wine. I saw the groaning, twitching motion of small, quinine-coloured muscles. The steam began to slither towards me, to creep through the cracks in the door, a foaming, expanding mass of jelly, a mass of twitching jelly-fish that were also spiders with black, hairy legs like levers marching closer and closer. An infernal warlike din started, the roar of machines, a myriad of screaming voices. Everything around me began to move. There was a mad rush of levers, spokes and pistons accompanied by the rabid, screaming cacophony of an invisible crowd of people. The machines started to shake me. The levers tore off my nightdress. I was naked. I was standing on a platform in the middle of a bawling, yelling mob and suddenly . . . the door . . . Seized with panic, I started up from my pillow in a cold sweat. A faint gleam of light shone through the gap between the floor and the door. Silence. The sound of his breathing – his wheezing. A shadow moved in the patch of light on the floor. "Whore . . ." I heard, "Whore . . . I'll teach her all right . . . I'll show her what respect means . . . So she thinks I'm drunk, does she?" The shadow swayed across the crack of light, seemed to topple, and then suddenly disappeared as the light burst in. My father was in the room, dressed only in his underpants. His legs stood wide apart, his knees almost giving way, swaying slightly. There was a blurred grin on his face. I clung to the blankets, rigid. Suddenly, I realised that this had all happened before. It was all exactly the same, except that before my mother had been there, she and I a twisted tangle of bodies clinging together on the bed, and this quinine-coloured figure swaying against the light of the door. And then my mother started screaming and her arms wrenched me into the darkness: "You leave that child alone! . . . Do what you want to me! Kill me if you want. Just leave the child!" But there was no one to hide me in the darkness now as my father bent over me, enveloping me in his alcoholic breath: "Shift over! I want to get in with you . . ." The scissors . . . the scissors on my bedside chair – they were still there from cutting up an old skirt for cleaning-rags . . . I groped in the dark and felt the cold steel in my hand. And as if all this were happening in some film that had nothing to do with me, I saw myself plunge the scissors blindly into the defenceless back above me. The flesh they entered was strangely bloodless, like clay. The horror that gripped me now was only the dread of not managing to kill him, of not succeeding with the first stab of the scissors. It was life or death for us both. And that meant I would die. But suddenly, just as I was about to strike, my father's body moved aside. Miraculously, he got up and staggered to the door. It shut behind him, extinguishing his unsteady, yellow body with the cone of light. An eternity passed, then I heard his snoring on the other side of the wall. Only then did the cold steel slip from my hand.

We were getting our reports at school. We had to go up and get them from the teacher's desk when our names were called out. I sat on my bench and waited for my turn. Since we were being called up in alphabetical order, my name, as usual, came last. The girl sitting next to me already had her report. She read it as far away from me as she could, as if to indicate that her report belonged to an altogether different category from anything I was likely to get. Its contents were evidently as much a secret as the maths answers which she always succeeded in hiding from me by barricading herself in behind a wall of arms and books whenever we were doing a test. I glanced over at the boys, who sat separately from the girls in their own row. Werner Lindner, whose father owned the photographer's on the market place, had just been called up to the front. His hair and clothes were smart like most of his classmates', some of whom would go on to work in their parents' businesses, while others would be leaving school that year, bound for banks and offices. According to my father, I was one of the latter. These were the last reports but one before leaving school. And it goes without saying that as I stood on the very brink of life as a German adult, on the threshold of life itself, a bottomless pit had opened before me. I held my report in my hand and looked down at its crushing contents. Not *one*, but four 4s were written in the squares opposite the subjects printed on the form. What was worse I had a 5 in German. The rest were 3s. Only in music did I have my usual 1, but that seemed merely to emphasise the awfulness of all my other marks. This meant I could be quadruply sure of being sent back to the convent, doubled again for getting a 5, and then there was the sheer mass of 3s which removed any doubt there might have been. Confronted with failure on this scale, it seemed to me that there must be some punishment even worse than convent, although I was unable to imagine one. Perhaps my father would send me to borstal. He had often threatened me with it when I was a child and his beatings had done nothing to tame or improve me. But whether convent or borstal, it made little difference in the end – both meant death. I sat on my school bench, aware of nothing but the ringing in my ears. I'd heard the same noise as a child when I'd lain in bed with high fever. It sounded like the high-pitched whine of telegraph poles in my head, and was intensified by the piercing April blue in the high, dome-shaped windows beside me. There was only one way I could go on living: I would have to take my life . . . Pills! yes, my mother's pills which were still in their tin on the dresser in my father's bedroom! I imagined him finding me when he came back from work later that afternoon . . . The ambulance, the German hospital, his remorse, his fear for my life . . . Something would be waiting there for me when I came round, something beyond my resurrection, and the thought of it gave me a feeling almost of glamour, of triumph . . .

Looking up from the certificate of my uselessness before me, I noticed to my alarm that everyone else in the class was packing up to go. I'd been so sunk in my own thoughts that I'd missed the bell. I quickly put my report in my bag and followed the others out into the corridor. All the other classes were pouring out at the same time, out into the Easter holidays which began that day. I pushed and jostled my way through the throng of pupils. I would have to hurry. There were only three hours left until my father came home.

"What are you doing this evening?" asked a girl with a green, velvet ribbon round her fox-red pony-tail, "I'm going dancing at the 'Linden'," replied her friend in a ringed pullover that hung down over her skin-tight jeans. I shoved past them, down the wide, worn steps of the entrance hall. I was surprised to find how warm it was outside. The muncipal gardens opposite the school buildings were all aglow with a rippling green that spilled out in different shades onto the street. The park offered the shortest route back to the "houses", and I would usually only take it when my father expected me straight back home after school; but today I was glad of the short-cut. My eyes only vaguely took in the green tresses of weeping-willows by the pond, where goldfish moved like the rays of mysterious lamps burning in the green gloom of a forest. I hurried on past the grottoes with their cascades of white jasmine-blossom, past a tree in full bloom, from which a warm breeze blew a shower of pink snow. A bright, dusty blanket of shadowless heat lay on the street at the other side of the park, and yet a cold shudder passed through my body. Suddenly, the thought of that fox-red pony-tail bouncing up and down the stairs in front of me stopped me in my tracks. Hadn't they said something about "dancing"? Wasn't it "this evening at the 'Linden'" they had said? They must have meant "The German Linden", a pub on Parade Square. I had often seen kids gathering outside it and heard dance music through the windows, the same hits that I'd heard on Wednesday evening request programmes on the radio. New vistas opened up before me, immediately dismissing all thoughts of dying from my mind. Lost in thought, I walked past the open windows of our yard. The "houses" meant nothing to me now. All I had to do was get changed in my father's flat. I decided to wear the deep blue, backless,

American taffeta dress, with a red patent leather belt and red high-heels to match. I lifted a five-mark note from the kitchen drawer where my father kept his money and, just for safety's sake, took my report from my schoolbag and hid it on the floor of my wardrobe. Then I left the flat – forever.

The High Street was packed with the usual bustle of weekend shoppers. The shops here sold almost everything you could possibly want, and yet I had never set foot in any of them. The inhabitants of the "houses" had their own, entirely exclusive shop. A clever German, an owner-occupier, whose misfortune it had been to have the "houses" built right in front of his somewhat secluded family residence, had set up shop in his own living room and was open twenty-four hours a day. After official closing-time you only had to knock on his front shutters and he'd hand you out your loaf of bread or pound of potatoes or whatever it was you'd forgotten, provided you still had credit with him. The drunks got their schnaps on Sundays and public holidays, too. Through us, the German shop-keeper had come into his own, personal, economic miracle. The destitution of the refugees from the East had turned his address into the least fashionable place in town. But by raking in the refugees' entire wages and benefit money in exchange for his wares, he had acquired capital returns on a scale far beyond even his wildest dreams.

I strolled up and down the High Street looking in shop windows, studying people's faces and clothes and the way they walked. My own get-up was unusual enough as it was, but it made me particularly conspicuous at that time of day, so that as I sauntered through the busy street I was painfully aware of the astonished, disapproving stares of the passers-by. Outside a butcher's, from which an enticing smell of roast meats wafted out onto the street, I suddenly noticed how hungry I was. I'd been in too much of a hurry to eat when I'd left home, and since I was generally incapable of forcing anything down my throat before I went to school in the morning, the borsch I had eaten the evening before had been the last thing to enter my stomach. The golden hands of the church-tower clock in the market place pointed to two o'clock; it was still ages until evening. And then a shocking thought jolted me to my senses. What would happen when my father came home from work in an hour's time and found I was missing? The question of what I was going to do all afternoon hadn't even crossed my mind. My father may even have decided to come home early, knowing my report would give him ample confirmation of his suspicions regarding my school conduct. By now, he would have noticed not only my own absence, but that of the five-mark note which I had taken from the drawer. He had probably already set out to look for me. Perhaps it had been clear to him for some time that today would be my day of reckoning. He would see my absence as proof of a degree of failure surpassing even his worst expectations. I began to walk. But I had no hope whatsoever of escaping my father. He would find me wherever I hid. He would track me down, even if it meant following me to a different planet. I turned off the High Street into a side alley. I felt a little safer in the semi-darkness between these narrow walls. Here, in this maze of streets at the heart of the German town, my father was even more of a stranger than I was. Here more than anywhere, my father and I were intruders. Here, our dreadful foreignness made us stick out like a sore thumb. I walked on and on, allowing the zig-zag of the half-timbering to guide me. The damp shadows along the walls sent a chill through my bones, and the noise of my quick footsteps on the rough cobbles was like a sacrilege. It was as though the obscene din of the "houses" were echoing in my every step, breaking a stillness that had been holy since time immemorial. Life at the "houses" was wide open for all to see. Everyone knew everything about everyone. But the Germans never let anything out. Everything in their lives was shrouded in genteel mystery, hidden behind heavy curtains and impenetrable faces, behind manners and expressions which I found impossible to grasp, and which always seemed to mean something different from what I thought. Here, too, the silence was perfect. Luckily for me, there was nobody about. Nobody behind those tightly closed, brightly polished windows seemed to notice me. Here and there a window was open a narrow crack, bringing the invisible interiors and unknown intimacies of German life tantalisingly close, so close I could almost smell them. In fact I really could smell something – German cooking. I felt a convulsion in my stomach and saw mountains of German food before me. I saw German *sauerkraut*, German dumplings, German sausages. I had visions of myself eating, wolfing down the entire contents of German pots and pans, eating the houses themselves with all their kitchens and sitting rooms and bedrooms, devouring all the Germans in Germany. I saw myself consume the whole lot of them and become something huge and bloated and German – Germany itself.

The alley I'd been walking down had brought me back out into the open. Without thinking, I had allowed myself to wander dangerously close to the "houses", and I now found myself beside the canal on the very road my father usually took home from the factory. Breathless from my brisk walk and looking around helplessly for a new escape route, an idea suddenly struck me. Of course! The cemetery on the other side of the canal, the cemetery where my mother lay! I would be quite safe from my father there. I'd be out of his reach. The cemetery lay within the forbidden realm of his silence, beyond a threshold he never crossed. My mother's spell was on the place. It was the only hiding place where I could be sure my father would never follow me. The cemetery really was a different planet!

For the first time in years. I was in the chapel of rest, looking at the closed coffins behind the glass panel. German death had become secretive too, secretive and uncanny under its closed lids and sumptuous garlands. Something was missing – that familiar odour, something mossy and sweetish emanating from the lifeless bodies on their beds of flowers and lace. Now there was no smell at all. The three closed coffins behind the glass were all frosty surface and polish. The tall, white candles which once had burned at the heads of the dead were cold and mute. Even the flowers on the wreaths seemed stiff and lifeless. It was as if real death had entered the chapel of rest, a kind of death I had never seen in the dead when I'd stood here as a child. The German dead had been more alive to me than the German living. They had shown me faces that were naked and accessible, faces which I had been able to study at length and without distraction on my way home from school every day: mouths, noses, hands. The glass panel in the chapel of rest had been my peep-hole into German life. And as the inevitable drew closer and closer, the magical ritual of my visits to the dead must also have been an occult means of preparing for the day when my own mother would be lying here behind this glass. But now there was no reason for me to stand here. The dead had become invisible, as invisible as the living behind their closed German doors and windows.

A stifling glare hung over the graves. Spring seemed to be exhausting its last drops of light on this afternoon, to be wasting itself in an act of will that would leave it utterly spent when the day was done. The hot, dusty smell of dry wreaths rose from the graves and merged with the smell of wilting flowers that seemed sated with the drowsy sleep of the dead beneath them. I stopped at a well and drank greedily. The cold musty water formed a painful lump in my empty stomach. Oppressed by the sultry heat, I at last reached my mother's grave. It was a heap of sand which still hadn't been levelled off. There were weeds growing out of it, thistles and the odd dandelion, some with heads that were already faded to a thin white fluff. And then the poor, worn gravestone with the Russian inscription my father had had engraved on it. The Russian lettering had been transformed by a German stonemason into a series of illegible hieroglyphs beside a Russian-Orthodox cross. Only my mother's name was in German, and the word "Russia", which stood out next to her date of birth. She had lived from 1920 to 1956, a Yevgenia Germanised in death, gaining the name Eugenie while losing the Russian feminine ending to her surname. Her Ukrainian origins, too, had fallen victim to my father's Germanised notion of "Russia". The whole thing was a total inconsistency, an embarrassing Russo-German patchwork; a neglected pile of sand surrounded by spruce German graves reminiscent of neat, owner-occupied homes, which were gradually being invaded, to the left and right of my mother's grave, by a creeping tangle of weeds.

How often had she rehearsed her death with me! It had started as one of those cruel games between mother and child which, though no longer funny, lingers on as a haunting shape beneath the surface, ready to pounce when you least expect it. Without a hint of warning, she would suddenly sink to the floor and play dead. When my desperate pleas to wake up remained unanswered, the game would take a more drastic turn. I would pull her hair, pinch her, prick her with needles. I wailed and screamed, wavering between the horror of failing, and revulsion at the monstrous way I was treating her, between frantic hope and helpless fear of the moment I longed for and yet dreaded, when my mother would cry out, her corpse-like rigor broken, and she would punish me for going too far and causing her pain. This punishment was the price I had to pay to redeem her, the sacrifice I made in return for her life. Although in the end even that wasn't enough to save her.

What was it like when it got really serious? How did my mother do it? How do you go into the water? The grey coat which they had found on the riverbank was the only explanation I had. She had taken off her coat, put aside the last thing that warmed and protected her on that October night by the river. It had been a warm day, I remembered, but a cold, almost frosty night. The hands of the kitchen clock had crept round and round in the growing stillness, and then – it must have been around midnight – I went over to the neighbours'.

She had removed her cumbersome coat and, in my mind's eye, she was standing on the bank in her green pullover with grey diamonds on its breast. There, in front of her, jet-black and cold as the autumn night – the river. A moment's hesitation perhaps? Did she take off her coat because it might get in the way if she decided to swim at the last moment? No, she had merely laid aside a bothersome article of clothing, an obstacle between herself and her goal. The coat was one of two signs she had left behind. There was the torn photograph on her bed, and the coat by the river. And then there was a third sign, a cross pencilled in on the calendar on the wall under the kitchen clock. A cross, in pencil, on Wednesday 10th October. Two coordinates: one for the time, one for the place. That was all. No farewell letter. No explanation. How long had she been silent? Since the postcard she had sent me at the farm in Belgium? A postcard sent to a ten-year-old child: "Nothing will ever be the same again . . ." From then until her death there had been about three months, one of which, the last, she spent with her child. For two, perhaps three, years her husband had been no more than a guest who dropped in between performances.

I ought to speak silently of her silence. Words on silence always fail to hit their mark. Just as all my words, all my sentences are my failed silence, the unentered silence which she dared enter. As long as I go on speaking. I am lying. "If you can say it's burning, it can't be burning very much!" I hold up the dull flame of my words to her silence, and it's like someone holding a match to a burning house.

I felt amazingly free at the time. A child whose father is away and whose mother is dead is usually entrusted to the care of another grown-up. But my mother wasn't dead. She was there. She existed, even though it was as if she weren't there, as if she didn't exist. I don't know what made her wait so long, why she kept on sitting there for a whole month on her kitchen chair, until the day with the cross on the calendar arrived. She simply sat on her kitchen chair and refused to speak. Overnight, I'd become utterly free. I could have had anything I wanted: the money in the drawer, sweets, as much chocolate as I could eat, the High Street, the yard, the meadows down by the river until late in the evening, school if I felt like it, and no school if I didn't. At night I tied a piece of string to my mother's foot and slept all night, holding the other end in my hand. I no longer dared stick pins in her, or pinch or bite her. The game was no longer a game. It was serious, and I knew it. "Mummy, say something!" That, shaking her hopelessly by the arm, was as far as I dared go. But her eyes stared through me into nothingness.

She was born during the Civil War, three years after the October Revolution. She was about sixteen when the mass arrests and murders began, the purges, the years of hunger. She was twenty-one and training to be a teacher when war broke out. Her father had died early. Her elder sister had been arrested and taken to a camp. She lost contact with her mother during the war years and never saw her again. In occupied Kiev, she worked for the German authorities in a so-called "Employment Office" which organised the deportation of Soviet workers to Germany. That meant certain death if Soviet troops recaptured the town. But the German occupation had meant death, too. If you didn't work for the occupation authorities, you didn't get any ration cards and then you starved to death. Such are the few sparse facts. The flight that followed lies hidden in darkness. She left with a man twenty years her senior, a man who, in the middle of a war, was prepared to leave his wife and two children behind him in the Soviet Union, a man whose background and education must have been quite foreign to her. They managed to reach Romania on a German warship. From there, they continued along the bombed railway tracks to Germany. Almost as soon as she arrived, a 24-year-old, handed over for forced labour in a Leipzig arms factory, she became pregnant. It was still wartime. The Soviet troops were coming closer. They had to flee westward again, towards more burning cities. When the flames had burnt themselves out, they found shelter in a disused shed. The war ended, and she gave birth to a daughter. Then they were arrested by the military authorities in the American zone of occupation for collaborating with the Germans, and under suspicion of espionage. Following their release from prison, there began an odyssey through German refugee camps, a series of failed attempts to emigrate to America, a marriage which had become hell before it had even started, and finally a refugee colony on the outskirts of a small German town, the end of the road. Another four years passed. She tried taking a job punching metal parts in a factory, but had to give it up after just a few days. She tried getting a divorce, but gave up half way through the court case. In the end she was alone after all, alone with her child. For she had been given a present of the very thing that she had struggled for in vain. Her husband had left of his own accord, become a singer in an émigré choir and hardly ever came home. He sent her money, not very often and not very much, but enough to get by on. When did she make her decision? She sent her child away for a whole year, or at least let her go, allowed it to happen. She was now absolutely alone, delivered of all bonds, all obligations. The countdown began, a final, dark year of which I know nothing, a year in which, despite everything, she still seemed to be waiting for her child to return. Or was she simply waiting for the day that she had crossed on the calendar, an ordinary Wednesday in October 1956? Perhaps that date related to some fateful day in her past. Perhaps it was the product of painstaking calculation. Perhaps it was all a kind of roulette, a lottery. Perhaps she had allowed herself a certain number of days after her child came back, had given herself one last chance. All perhaps, perhaps . . . . It may all have been quite different.

The day with the cross on the calendar arrives, and with it a miracle. The mother speaks. She speaks all by herself, without the child doing anything to provoke her. The child has long since given up pulling at the mother's arm and begging for an answer. The child only speaks to herself, out of habit or out of fear. She talks and talks, tells stories, anything that comes into her head. On this day, too, she's been as insistent as a waterfall, talking as if possessed, talking to the pot on the stove in which she is cooking herself a meal after school, talking to the dishes in the cupboard, talking to the walls, talking into thin air, and suddenly she gets an answer. It's as if the chair to which the mother has been frozen for four weeks has itself started to speak. She says only five words: "You won't be going tomorrow." The child was prattling on about the school outing the next day, and that was the mother's reply: "You won't be going tomorrow." What does she mean? That the child won't be going with her to the river? Or is she hoping that her long-forgotten voice will achieve some breakthrough? Is she hoping that she will hear her own words and will reject the course of action they imply, or that the child's resistance will move her? Is this her last attempt at a provocation? Or is it her way of finally confirming everything to herself, sealing it with the stamp of her own voice, while at the same time leaving behind a hidden message to prepare the child for what is to come? The provocation works. The mother's words drive the child to distraction, into a fit of hatred. Because the child has understood without knowing it. She has understood everything, and now she wants to go on the school outing more than anything else in the world. The child shouts and begs and flies into a rage and throws herself at her mother's feet: "I want to go on the school outing!" But her mother says only one more word: "No."

She leaves the house long before dark. The day is sunny but quite cool, so she puts on a coat. One of the neighbours sees her that afternoon wandering about in the meadows down by the river, or rather walking about – as if she were out for a walk. It's the last anyone sees of her. Nobody sees her wandering about aimlessly in the twilight, waiting for darkness to fall. Perhaps she is extremely aware of this dying light, the last changing of light and dark that she will ever witness. She has already chosen the spot.

I follow her as far as the self-hatred which pushes me across the threshold of my own fear, fear of self-destruction, fear of physical pain. I am going to destroy the thing that is making my life hell. I am going to wipe out this indestructible torment of self. I am going to murder my own murderer. That is as far as I go. Every suicide is alone in the end. Because the final step is outside the ken of the living. She has taken off her coat, folded it carefully and laid it on the damp grass of the river bank. This final gesture, her hand brushing across the surface of the coat, reveals the degree of care and precision that she has reserved for death. Perhaps she stands there for a while, staring into the black current. Perhaps there is a moment's hesitation. Perhaps she thinks of the child she is leaving to a terrible fate, to a world she, at that very moment, is declaring unacceptable, to a father to whom she once offered her life in exchange for the child's safety. No, that's not what she thinks! The child was her ultimate enemy, after all, the final hurdle, a piece of string tied to her foot, keeping her in this hell. She had lain in bed at night struggling with this enemy. She had stood beside the sleeping child's bed, had thought about taking the child with her . . . I can't follow her any further. The first step into the water, shallow still at the bank, but piercingly cold, even if the frozen body no longer feels it. The first step, the second, the third . . . How did Paul Celan drown himself in the Seine? How did Virginia Woolf do it? And why choose water?

"Death by drowning is death by suffocation. However, contrary to what is often thought, this is not brought about by water entering deep into the respiratory tract, but by a spasmic contraction of the larynx which is stimulated by the invasion of even a small quantity of water and leads to the sealing of the air passages. At the same time, a person who drowns swallows a considerable amount of water, so that his specific gravity increases, causing him to sink. In fact, death by drowning takes only a few minutes."

She has a sick heart. Perhaps she doesn't get very far into the icy water before the cold gives her a fatal shock. Perhaps this is what she thought would happen. She has a collapse. And the rest? Everything else happens automatically. Or else she keeps on walking, step by step, right out to the bottomless depths in the middle of the river. She doesn't feel the roots and the sharp stones under her feet even though she has lost her shoes. Her strength fails her, and at last the current drags her away. But then, just as the flood overwhelms her, her instincts resist it . . . the spasm, the body's final defence against this invading foreign element; flailing arms, the reflex action of hands grabbing out for something to hold onto, anything, any substance to pit against this smothering end-of-all-substance. She can't swim, but fear of death makes her try. Perhaps, for an instant, her will to live asserts itself over everything else. Perhaps she makes a last, desperate effort to stay alive. But it's too late.

Versions of the truth. Attempts at a reconstruction. Stabs in the dark. For a few weeks after her mother's funeral the child wakes up at the same time every night. She wakes in the dark, hurries into the kitchen and switches on the light, though she knows very well what the clock on the wall will say. Thirty-seven minutes past three. Had this been the time of her mother's death, had it really been her dead mother waking her, as the child believed, then her mother must have wrestled with herself for a long time. Perhaps she was a hair's breadth away from coming home. The post-mortem report gives the time of death as between midnight and the early hours of the morning . . .

She finally arrived in Germany. The German cemetery embraced her into its community. There was no resistance. Nobody there raised their voice. She had attained in death what in life had always eluded her.

It was getting cold and shadowy. The sun had sunk behind the high wall of cypresses at the far end of the cemetery, and the evening was still a long way off. I walked up and down the rows of graves and whiled away the time by readi inscriptions. I shivered. Hunger was a little lizard away at the walls of my stomach. It seemed so strange that Germans died, too. They, too, were forced to contend with this, the greatest defeat. It meant they actually had something in common with my mother! But there was nothing scandalous about German death, whereas I had always been ashamed of my mother's Russian death and never knew what to say when I was asked what she died of. Such a young woman, too! The unhappy circumstances of her death had rubbed off on me, plaguing me with a shameful sense of defeat. But it wasn't her defeat. It was mine.

I read the gravestones, letting the names, dates, places of birth and occupations form into stories. I saw faces and landscapes. I heard voices. The word "Sudetenland", where a Helene Hein had been born, suggested the hazy blue of a river winding its way through a valley of birch trees. The name Richard Graf, born in 1896 in the Fichtel mountains, conjured up a weather-beaten old man with his hat pulled firmly down over his leathery face, his back bent like the trunks of giant fir trees whose heads had bowed for thousands of years in the storms that swept through the Fichtel mountains. German warriors marched up before a uniform row of grey head-stones, a German guard of honour consisting of a lance-corporal, reservists, infantrymen, bombardiers and sergeants. The lance-corporal shot his arrow right to the heart of his young German fiancée. A choir of bombardiers sang in mighty German canon. The reservists had few reservations when it came to going to the front against enemy Russia. They had been dead for almost half a century, all of them young men, almost children, all of them killed in action in the same year, in some war I knew nothing about. I inspected the ranks and selected a German bridegroom. It had to be a lance-corporal, and his name had to be dark-sounding, had to go well with dark hair and dark eyes, with a pale, painfully beautiful face.

"Achim Uhland," I read, "Lance-Corporal, 1898 – 1917". I thought of the German chaplain I'd fallen so hopelessly in love with at the convent. I remembered an occasion after I'd been permitted to go to Communion, when I had bitten my lip so viciously that it had bled. I had offered this hurt lip with its red drop of blood to the chaplain at the communion rail, as a silent token of my forbidden love. And he had accepted my offering. He had taken the white communion-cloth from his arm and carefully and earnestly dabbed the blood from my lip. Only then had he placed the Host on my tongue in a manner which seemed to me to return my love. From then on I had tacitly consented to being his. I had become a third party, admitted to the secret union between the Catholic Christ and the German chaplain with the dark eyes and pale, painfully beautiful face, a beauty which hurt because one could never be part of it. Achim Uhland bowed before me in his lance-corporal's uniform: "May I have the pleasure of this dance?" I remembered dancing at the convent. We were permitted to dance on special occasions once or twice a year. We only danced with each other, of course. The male sex was strictly banned. I remembered waltzes and polonaises which Sister M. had put on the old-fashioned gramophone for us in the refectory. She had joined in, too, and her bouncing, swelling skirts and veil were like the plumage of a huge, black bird that would suddenly become a vehicle for the wrath of God. One never felt safe from Sister M.'s infamous "bad moods". This was the official term for her inevitable, and yet totally unpredictable, fits of bad temper. It was said that decades of institutionalised life had ruined her nerves. At the drop of a hat, her cheerfulness would turn into a storm of rage, into thunder and lightning that crashed down out of the blue. She would walk up and down the rows, her hand slapping out at our ducking heads as if on a spring. Or she'd thrash us with the wooden beads of her rosary, an instrument of chastisement that always hung ready at her waist.

As the afternoon drew in and the German "Linden" came closer and closer, I began to feel uneasy. I felt so dreadfully far away from the normal life of German boys and girls. In fact I knew nothing about their lives or what they did. I didn't even understand their language. Did I really dare take all my abominably cloistered and Russian otherworldliness straight to the heart of their utterly strange world and be confronted with everything that made me so foreign? A fat old woman passed me with a watering can in her hand. Apart from myself, she seemed to be the only visitor left in the cemetery. She gave me a menacing glare, and I saw the figure of someone in a taffeta dress bobbing up and down in her bluish, jelly-like eyes. How odd I must have looked, in the cemetery at such a late hour! The cypresses at the edge of the cemetery had turned dark grey and a final, violet shimmer of dusk lay upon the gravestones. I still didn't dare leave the cemetery. I saw the faint outlines of a bench. To my alarm, I thought I recognised my father sitting on it. But it was nothing, a phantom of the twilight air. My legs had begun to hurt and a surging nausea overcame me, filling my mouth with a gluey substance that stuck my tongue to the roof of my mouth. I had come across some green leaves in the grass by the wall of the cemetery. They had tasted like sorrel, but the more I thought about them, the greater became my dismay. Perhaps the leaves were poisonous. Perhaps this was the punishment for all my ill deeds. I felt the stuff of dead bodies inside me, as if I had swallowed their putrefaction along with the leaves that had grown on their remains. Or perhaps what I had inside me was not sorrel at all, but the sweet flesh of the dead themselves. A cold shudder, went through me. Exhausted, I sank onto the bench. All at once, I saw before me Ada, the grey Alsatian bitch that had belonged to my father. He had Ada put down one day, and I never found out why . . . I could see her in the distance, bounding towards me. Wild with joy, I ran to meet her. I knelt down on the ground and was about to throw my arms around her when I noticed there was something terribly the matter with her. She was writhing and squirming, howling and whimpering. She was in pain, but I couldn't see what was wrong with her. I searched desperately for the cause of her suffering, but found nothing. Then it dawned on me that her torment was my fault. It was because of the way I had tortured the dog as a child, conducting cruel experiments to test my power over her. I had wanted to know how much the animal was prepared to endure for me. I had abused it with sticks and pieces of broken glass, hesitating between fear of the dog's revenge and my sadistic desire for some extreme proof of its love for me, a proof which, to my astonishment, it always delivered in its mute affliction. I now recognised the green piece of glass that I had used as an instrument of torture. It was fixed around the dog's nose in a kind of ring. I saw its sharp edges lodged in the dog's flesh and I knew there was nothing I could do to alleviated the animal's whining and suffering. An eerie, unnatural darkness fell. I was holding the whimpering dog in my arms. I had to carry it through an underground system of winding, labyrinthine tunnels in order to get to a doctor, but the further I went, the more lost I became. Desperate, I tried to get back on the path, but it grew fainter and fainter, more and more confusing. All of a sudden, I spied a bright point of red light marking the end of the darkness. It was a tiny, purple flame that danced to and fro, disappearing for a moment, then flickering up again. Horror-stricken, I realised where I was. Like an insect paralysed by the cold, I was lying on a bench in the cemetery. I was completely incapable of moving. And the horror didn't let up. Everything in me seemed to have stopped. My heart had stopped beating. I was no longer breathing. There was no doubt about it – I was dead. The pills that I had swallowed in order not to have to die had killed me. Something had gone wrong. Nobody had rescued me. And so this was death, wanting to scream, and not being able to. Wanting to run, but not being able to. Frozen terror. A silent scream, lasting for ever. A breath of cold air brushed over my skin, a stir in the atmosphere, releasing me and bringing me to my feet with a start. I had no idea how long I'd been sleeping on the bench. Perhaps it was already late at night. The graveside lamp flickering in the hazy distance was the only visible thing in the dark cemetery. Panic seized me yet again. The cemetery would be locked at this time of night. To get out I was going to have to climb over the gates. I struggled free of the paralysis that gripped me, as if this were my last chance of wresting myself from the clutches of the dead, and started to run. I ran from the cold that froze me to the marrow, and they all came running after me: the one-eyed Czech with his concertina; the lascivious Bulgarian on his crutches; Wilfried, whose torn body had lain beside the railway track. Ada whom I'd tortured to death was after me. My mother was after me, dragging me down to the bottom of the river where I was eternally guilty for her death, guilty for not waking her with my pin-pricking and biting. Lance-corporal Achim Uhland, my dead fiancé, was after me. I ran between trees and bushes, twigs brushing my face like the feathers of some huge, wet, black bird as I followed the only track I could make out in the darkness, the narrow, moonlit band of a gravel path. I ran for my life.

Perhaps I still haven't said in this story that I was happy then. I was happy because I "lived life outwardly", as Fernando Pessoa says of his childhood. And everything inward that I have put in the story comes from the inner life I have now, but didn't have then. "I enjoyed everything, even the things I had no reason to enjoy. I lived life outwardly, and my suit of clothes was spotless and new. What more can a person ask for who must die and doesn't know it and is holding his mother's hand? There was once a time when I enjoyed all this, which is why it is only perhaps now that I realise quite how much I did enjoy it. I went to mass as if entering a great mystery, and I left mass as if lighting upon a forest glade. That is how it really was and that, truly, is how it still is. Only an unbelieving adult, one whose soul still remembers everything and weeps, only he is fiction and distress, confusion and the cold grave. Yes, what I am now would be unbearable if I could not remember what I once was."

I was happy then, and that is what I am trying to remember now. In fact, I was happier than other people, for I lived life more "outwardly" than they did. I was on the outside of life, and everything outside me was above me, and because it was above me it was better than me. So everything was better than me, and I therefore had an unlimited capacity to believe in things. I was less limited altogether than other children, for they had begun to question things whereas I was the child who was holding her mother's hand. I knew nothing of mortality. I lived without any knowledge of my own, defenceless against the knowledge of others, against the things that entered my mind, against myself. I lived in a paradise in which I had no identity, in which I was in harmony with everything around me. I distinguished myself neither from good nor from bad, neither from other people nor from myself. I lived without the inward division that refracts the self into countless different selves. And if it is true that this inner difference begins with birth, then I am not speaking here as an unborn person, but as one who has been born and refracted countless times, just as all things born and all things that speak are refracted. I was unborn then, however, and therefore intact. And yet even now, I can sense the presence of something unborn within me, for the unborn is always present in everything. But in me it is an abscess that has never burst, whose contents are unknown to me. What it contains may be fatal, and I am afraid of death. I am so afraid of death that I die countless deaths, deaths that lie in wait for me every second of the day. Can one die in order to be born? Where is the midwife that would help? Psychology has exhausted itself reproducing the structures of a civilisation that is bent on self-destruction. Why has God given up his midwifery? I simply don't know. I write because it is dark.

I write of going dancing for the first time, and being happy. I was happy because I was dancing, because *he* was there in the dance hall at "The German Linden", because he could see me. I was happy because I was visible to someone at last. I danced with the German craftsman, but for his eyes only, the eyes of someone sitting in semi-darkness among the empty tables and chairs, someone who wasn't dancing with me and who had attracted my attention precisely because he didn't dance with anyone. He seemed to be there only to show me that he existed and would always be beyond my reach. He was no more than a dark outline in a world of dancing couples, a hall of people who were stamping and swinging to the rhythms of the latest waltzes and rock'n' roll, a sea of figures under the surging play of lights, merged into one quivering, throbbing, sweating mass of hot bodies that were pressed together in close, swaying couples on the dance floor. And there I was, immersed in it all! It was like plunging into a jungle of tropical lianas. I felt wet sideburns and knees pressing themselves against me. I breathed in the smell of sweet Brylcreem, beer and sweat. Little waves of nausea seemed to be coming from the bottom of a chasm that yawned inside me, waiting for me to fall. I was already teetering on the edge. Beneath the tattered finery of my dancing gear, I was at the mercy of my intoxication and fever, my dizziness and thirst. At last the German craftsman released me from his grasp. I was free to move in *his* gaze. I felt myself grabbed by the rhythm of rock'n' roll, a body-language I understood at once, grasping it straight away as a language which was mine beyond everything German and Russian. It was a means of self-expression which allowed me to participate, even if only for the short duration of a dance. I was part of a metabolic process, a system of fluid exchange that united me with everyone else. But the only one I really desired was one who spurned all that, an armour-clad prince who sat aloof. Cold and beautiful in his black leather jacket with its silver, spiky studs, he had a pale Achim-face and dark Uhland-eyes. He was an outsider like me, but one for whom that was choice, a source of nobility that made him the secret sovereign of this kingdom, since he was the only one capable of rejecting it. His standoffishness made him look like a younger, German version of my father, and he was also my own male German counterpart, an outcast, an outlaw like myself, but one who had turned the tables. I had found him at last, and now I was waiting for him to take me, to take

possession of this fallow land, this no-man's-land that was me.
From that evening onwards, he was my reason for living, my
sure foundation, but also my abyss. My searchlight had come
to rest on him. I must give him a name, an invented name of
course. I've had to invent everything in this story, because
everything is irretrievably lost. Even I am an invention. So let
me call him Achim Uhland, because this name was personified for me in him. It was the name of a fantasy, for which a
fortuitous glance at a gravestone had merely provided the
appropriate sound. I have no idea where this fantasy began.
Who knows where anything begins? But my searchlight had
picked out a nineteen-year-old boy who had just been let out
of borstal, a kid who "cracked" cars and vending machines.
Like me, he had no mother and a violent drinker as a father. I
followed him. I pursued him. The darker my life, the further I
followed him into an ever greater darkness, into the increasingly impenetrable thicket where this fantasy had once
begun. He was the ultimate in inaccessibility and therefore
the supreme incarnation of the world itself. He was my father
and Germany in one. He was Achim Uhland – dead. I could
not have found anything more remote.

The other boy was called Hans and was Achim Uhland's
friend. His searchlight had come to rest on me that evening at
the German "Linden". He had made it quite plain that he
wanted me, and although I had been yearning for something
like this to happen, and seen it as my only hope of salvation, I
suddenly realised I hated him for it. For I immediately saw
him as something that wanted to possess me. I probably felt
some part of my father was trying to get at me through him. I
would probably have felt the same way about anyone who had
fallen in love with me. It wasn't someone who offered himself
to me that I was after, but someone who withdrew. I wasn't
interested in presents, but in attaining the unattainable. It was

the story of all my woes. Love as a present was useless to me. It had no value. It was worse than that. It was like the feeling of having a rash or a deformity. Love felt like this to me because even the first tentative ray of love that touched me immediately revealed the complete absence of love in my life, revealed the terrible insecurity which made love feel so dangerous to me. It was the danger of my own extinction that I felt; and that, after all, was what I was running away from. Perhaps all this was the deeper meaning of the way Achim Uhland looked at me in the "German Linden" that night. Perhaps this was the affinity between us, an affinity that would separate me from him forever. On the other hand, perhaps there was something much simpler separating me from him, or at least something that intensified what set me apart from him anyway. "I see," he said on hearing my name, "so you're from the houses, are you?" My shame flared up, a burning stigma for all to see. Now I was truly visible! I blushed awkwardly under his expert gaze, which seemed to have picked me out from the rest and stamped me as a reject. But presently I forgot about it and danced with Hans instead. It was through Hans that I was sitting at Achim Uhland's table. Hans's blunt and violent love for me was another thing that seemed to come between me and Achim Uhland, and yet it was also my only point of contact with him. The script of my approaching fiasco was written by events at the German "Linden" that evening. The scenario could now unfold. I had crossed the threshold and there was no going back. I had stepped out into the world and, though I was light years away from arriving anywhere, retracing my steps was impossible. I had to cross a precipitous chasm. Luckily for me I was unaware of this. Had I known, I should have fallen like a sleepwalker who wakes to find himself looking down into the fatal depths beneath him. I shall have to tell a story which I already know is untellable. It is a story of darkness. I shall only be able to tell it by bringing light to that darkness, but then it will be a different story. I cannot throw light on the darkness without light entering it. I cannot re-enter the darkness myself. In order to tell this story, I shall have to stand in the shadows. I shall have to tell it from a twilight zone, as if I had just woken up on the roof of a tower block. I shall have to tell the kind of story where you know what's going to happen before it even starts, whose plot is banal and inevitable, a boring story – as boring as life itself. My task will be to salvage its secret, to redeem the traces of a secret left on all things, the traces of a darkness we cannot speak about.

I awoke in a bed of icy darkness. It occurred to me that this was the second such awakening in one night, and sure enough the only thing that I could make out in the dark was a tiny flickering light, just like the one I had seen on waking in the cemetery. But I was quite clearly not outside now. I was no longer lying on the flat surface of a bench. Instead, there was something sharp and uneven under me, something painful sticking into my frozen flesh. The air was subterranean. Perhaps I was locked away in some underground cell. There was a musty, crypt-like smell, and I had the strange sensation of lying on rubble. My mouth was full of sand or earth. My body felt utterly rigid. Once again, it seemed that I had woken up dead, only this time I was already buried. But then, what was that red dot of light which I could see above me in the dark? How could I be looking at a graveside candle? How could I see anything at all if I were under the earth? Hadn't I escaped from the cemetery? Hadn't I climbed over the locked gate, its sharp, claw-like spikes tearing a triangle in my dress? Hadn't I cut my knee jumping down? And hadn't I eventually got to the dancehall at the German "Linden" where I had met Achim Uhland? Or had I met him in this cemetery? And had my whirl of happiness and light been merely a dream between two periods of darkness, a festival of the dead in which I was also dead and had met my German fiancé, Lance-Corporal Achim Uhland, who would now be lying somewhere close by under his own gravestone? Or did I really go to the

German "Linden"? And what of the rest of that evening, which I now saw before me in a series of increasingly clear images? Had it really happened then, or was it all a dream? Had I really roared through the dark streets of the town on the back of Achim Uhland's moped, my arms clasped firmly around his black leather jacket with its cold silver studs? Could I really feel it reverberating in my ears, the booming howl of the engine screaming through the sleeping streets like a hurricane? It was like a bomb going off in the holy stillness of the German night as the moped raced from one street to the next, zig-zagging through the whole town at an unholy, break-neck speed, until I was set down on the kerb by the "houses", a kerb so high that I had perched on it as a child with my feet dangling down, as if on a watchtower. Dazed, the wind still roaring in my ears, I suddenly felt him take me in his arms and kiss me . . . I stood there for a moment, flabbergasted, wondering what on earth had happened to my lips, while the noise of the moped dwindled and was finally gone in the darkness. Though the day had been relatively warm, it was now one of those cold April nights when buds freeze on the trees. I immediately saw the hopelessness of my situation. There was nothing I could do but go back home and hope for my father's mercy. There was no mercy out here. I shivered with fear and cold under my thin dress. The intense cold of my ride through the night now caught up with me in a concentrated blast, lashing my body like a whip and leaving me so weak that I felt that the yawning chasm which had been waiting for me while I danced at the German "Linden" was about to open up and swallow me.

Luckily, the outer door of the house wasn't locked. I managed to get into the stairwell and ring my father's door. For a long time, I heard nothing. For a moment, I thought my father was dead. He must be dead, since he hadn't come out and struck me dead there and then. For a moment, the thought of his possible death gave me a final, overwhelming sense of hope. I went on pressing the door bell, and the fiercer and more urgently I rang, the more my fear of the endless darkness of the night outside grew. Added to this was the fear that my father might still appear, which, after my violent assault on his sleep, was bound to end in my physical destruction. Suddenly, I heard my father's footsteps inside the flat. But it didn't matter what happened to me now. I was far too exhausted to feel afraid. His voice came from behind the door: "What do you want? Get lost! Away with you! There's no room in my house for a whore!"

I tried to get into the attic, and then into the cellar, where I knew there was a lot of old junk, a warm jumble of rags, cardboard boxes and wooden boards. These were all our worldly possessions, dragged along from one refugee camp to the next, from one compulsory residence to the other, until we had finally got to the "houses" and the German charity "Caritas" had presented us with an assortment of objects that provided a semblance of real furniture, so that the rubbish we had lived with up until then had been relegated to the cellar, where we suspiciously hoarded it and allowed it to rot all these years. But I tried in vain. I wasn't able to get into the attic either, where I'd hoped to find a place among the lumber our neighbours had stored there. The only door I found unlocked was the door of our coal cellar, a kind of boarded, under-ground cavern. After a while, I got up from the ice-cold floor of the cellar and sought a slightly warmer bed on a pile of coal. I plunged into a pitch-black, deathlike sleep, and on waking, saw the tiny red eye of an illuminated light-switch staring at me from the wall . . .

It was impossible to tell how long I'd been asleep, how long I'd been lying in this subterranean cold. In fact I didn't feel the cold at all. My body was quite numb. I could feel myself drifting away again. I felt I was going back in time into something like the glittering lights I'd danced beneath at the German "Linden". I had visions of tropical landscapes, fantastic scenes, constantly changing like a kaleidoscope. Later, I found there was one image I remembered particularly well. It was a mountain that glowed in the colours of precious stones. Celestial music came from these colours, and I felt I was part of the coloured sounds, too. And it was like something which I had experienced before, when I had merged with the green ringing in the river. But this time the wolves had found me and leapt on me. I could feel them tearing my lungs out. A weak ray of sunlight had squeezed its way in through the hatch in the roof of the cellar. It seemed to have touched my body, bringing back the vital functions of my organs. A raging fit of coughing tore at my chest and shook me back to my senses. Moving was like bending a piece of cast iron into human shape, limb by limb, until at last I was back on my feet, swaying like some contraption balanced on two frozen stakes. Voices and other sounds mingled with the daylight and seemed to come pouring down a funnel from the yard. Apparently, it was warm and sunny again outside. I had another fit of coughing, bringing up lumps of black dirt that had caked the insides of my lungs. Coal dust had entered every pore of my body. I was black from head to foot. A dreadful thought occurred to me. I couldn't possibly leave the cellar and go out like this into the light and warmth. How could I let myself be seen in such a state? Once again, my only hope lay in begging for my father's mercy. I would have to try ringing his door a second time.

One of the two rooms in our flat had always been "my room", even when my mother was alive. But this room had done nothing to improve my self-confidence. On the contrary, it had merely contributed to my humiliation. I had never wanted it anyway. To me it was just another part of the despicable "houses", with the added ignominy that I was forced to call it my own. Even if somebody had offered me a palace there, I should have turned it down. But my room had little in common with a palace. It was dark and dingy, and the bare stone walls and concrete floor made it ice-cold in winter. There were a few shabby articles of furniture, a wardrobe, a table and chair, and a fold-away camp-bed covered with torn Red Cross blankets. It was like a prison cell. I was banished to this desolate hole every day to do my homework. I was told to look after it and keep it clean. In short, I was supposed to see it as a privilege and be grateful for it. In fact I hated my parents for giving me this "privilege", just as I hated them for everything I had to do and be and experience because of them. "Parents" was a word that crumbled the moment it entered my mouth, a word I found impossible to utter. It united two entirely incompatible principles: father and mother. I could not imagine two people more distant from one another. They were opposites, and the only possible product of their unity was deadly hatred, of which I was the incarnation.

There was a brief period in my life, immediately after my

return from the convent, when I was quite happy to have this room. It was my first experience of anything I could call my own after years of having the personality drained out of me night and day in a community enforced through an endless series of dormitories, study rooms, refectories and class-rooms. There had been no privacy at all at the convent. Not even my body had belonged to me. It was as if the whole lot of us had been lumped together in a pot, crushed to a pulp, diluted, and then boiled to some ethereal vapour. For a time, I was happy to be the daughter of a real father again, too. It made me feel I'd been given back my self. I tried to make this self attractive by making my room attractive. I was allowed two pieces of golden lining material to hang up as curtains. I found some old wooden shelves in the cellar and gave them a coat of the Prussian blue that I had chosen specially at the paint shop. Prussian blue! The mysterious world of the Germans in my very own room! It was a colour I had heard of in novels, in sagas of wealthy German families whose lives I tried to picture in respectable villas in great, distant cities by a sea of Prussian blue. And on the shelf, I kept an old greenish copper tin with a medieval castle engraved on its lid. The tin contained an old friend of mine, my mother's sewing things, and the blood, sweat and tears I had invested in German needlework classes. It contained my pincushion with the blue and red satin, and the cross-stitch at which I'd always failed so miserably. I had been hopeless at all the German embroidery, knitting and sewing that we got for homework. I had felt so lonely when I'd had to sit down to crochet an insert for a pillow case, like those the Germans kept in linen cupboards smelling of starch and white-scented blossom; or when I'd had to darn the heel of a brown stocking which the handicrafts teacher had undone for the fourth time. I'd ask my mother to help me, but she was at a loss, too. In fact she had no more talent for the world of

German embroidery and knitting than I had. The world of German female dexterity and virtue tolerated nothing but perfection, and our fingers simply weren't up to it.

We didn't seem to be up to much at all. Every day was a failure. And there was no improvement as the years went by; it just got worse and worse. Germany and all its efficiency got further and further away. It seemed to want to disassociate itself from us. It became stranger and stranger, more and more incomprehensible, until one day we found that it was ourselves we couldn't understand. We had turned into ghosts, incomprehensible spectral figures with guilty looks that became increasingly guilty the less we understood, the more our efforts were in vain.

Why didn't we just leave? Why didn't I leave? What was it I wanted in this country? I know what it was. I wanted my self back. Yes, I still belong to you people. And I shall stay here until I've managed to wrench myself from your grip.

My window looked out onto a kind of wasteland, a mixture of heath and slag. It was a no-man's-land, a death-zone designed to keep us apart from the Germans. It was literally the end of the road, the world's-end. Beyond here, there were only the river meadows, the gravel-pits and forests. There were only the huts of the gypsies, to which there was no road, only a narrow path leading along the dried-up bed of a canal. I'd been happy out there once. "Out there" had belonged to us, to the refugee children. It had been the scene of all our wildest adventures, a gift presented to us by a people who wanted to keep us outside their reconstructed urbanity. They had given us children a wilderness, a backward, primitive piece of nature which they had no use for, and this had become our continent. Out there, we roamed throughout the seasons in our hordes. We banded together in tribes and gangs. We were Mongolian horsemen in the dusty heat of the steppes. We laid waste to rubbish dumps and scrap heaps. We hacked paths through bushes, undergrowth and nettles as if they were tropical jungles full of unsuspected dangers. We were warlike nomads among the dunes of the gravel-pits. We attacked caravans in the desert, and were attacked ourselves. We were stranded with broken masts on the uninhabited coasts of the riverbanks, where we were ambushed by cannibals shooting a hail of poisoned arrows. We bivouacked on the dried up bed of the canal and nourished ourselves from the bitter fruits of the wild pear tree, or by picking sorrel and robbing birds' nests. We occupied territories and built towns out of rubble and refuse, and fought great battles in the name of these towns. We were hostile armies, reunited to form one nation. We were driven on by insatiable appetites through eerie twilights and into forbidden darkness. We were exhausted and dirty, but happy.

One day though, I came upon something uncanny out there. I had been wandering about alone and had strayed so far from home that I had eventually got lost. I didn't recognise any of the landmarks. Wherever I looked there were just the same fields and woods. Suddenly, I found myself standing in front of a fence, behind which there were some miserable-looking, half-dilapidated farm buildings. Although it was a hot summer's day, there was a fine cloud of smoke rising from the chimney, the only sign that the farm was inhabited. And then a weird figure appeared from the bushes behind the fence. I had never seen anything like it. A human being that looked like an animal; an indefinable, bloated creature, disfigured through neglect beyond all recognition, standing behind the fence with a stick in his hand, gaping at me with swollen eyes. There were various liquids oozing out of his mouth, nose and eyes. It was impossible to make out a face behind the scabs and grease, behind the tangle of hair and straw which grew on

his head like some matted fleece. I stood there rooted to the
spot, unable to run away, and the dribbling, grinning creature
behind the fence gawped and gawped. The stick had fallen
out of his hand, and he was pressing his hands and face to the
wire mesh of the fence, gurgling blissfully and licking the
rusty wire, which turned his saliva brown. And all the while, he
stared at me intently with his bloodshot eyes. I began to feel a
growing horror. I still couldn't move. But it wasn't my fear of
being attacked that prevented me from running. I was
spellbound by the sight of the bestial neglect into which the
imbecile had fallen. It was the absence of anything re-
cognisably human in what was so obviously a human being.
Beyond us, beyond "the houses", were the gypsies. And
beyond the gypsies, as far away as possible from human
society, there was just this imbecile. He grinned and slavered
and I saw that he was overwhelmed by a craving to get close to
me. His constant licking and sucking at the rusty mesh made it
look as if he were trying to eat up the fence, the only barrier
between him and me. He jumped up and down, making little
convulsive barking noises and banging his hands on the wire.
It was as if he were demonstrating how happy he was to have
found another living being on the other side of the fence, and
as if he were trying to attract the attention of this other being
so that it would acknowledge his own presence and share in
his babbling happiness at this mutual recognition. I had lost
all track of time. I seemed to be looking through a hole in the
air into the abyss of an undreamt-of reality. Suddenly the
figure of a man emerged from the shadowy farm buildings
and I heard an angry, menacing voice which seemed to be
directed at the imbecile. As if my feet had been waiting for this
signal, they suddenly became uprooted and I began to run. It
felt as if I were running from myself, as if I had to escape from a
side of myself I had never seen before, a side that was obscure

and neglected, the bestial pariah side that only this imbecile had been able to reveal to me. I ran straight across country, through ploughed fields and over ditches, until at last I saw the blue, shimmering band of the river in the distance, and knew the way home lay upstream.

Ever since I was a child, I had always spent as much time as I could outside. I had only ever returned home because I had to. My parents' home was a constraint, a constant repressive force, like the convent which had been my prison for five years and which itself had been merely an extension of the isolation and confinement I had suffered in the refugee ghettos. I had never lived among ordinary human beings, only among subhumans from the East and among the superhuman Catholic clergy. What I was really doing was waiting. I had been waiting for as long as I could remember, waiting for something that would mark the beginning of a life, the beginning of myself. Waiting had become my identity; waiting and the desire to escape. I could at least escape to the yard, or to freedom with the others in the gravel-pits. The only happiness I felt in the vicinity of the "houses" was when I was playing with the other refugee children. The "houses" were a territory to which I had been banished, and only my adventures with the others allowed me to forget this. I suffered from a constant longing to be somewhere else. It was like my mother's homesickness. This place of exile was our common affliction, and she and I shared a continuous, agonising desire to be somewhere far away. Of course, it wasn't my mother's Ukraine that I longed for. It was a mysterious place called Germany, which wanted nothing to do with me, a place right outside our door, directly beyond the walls and fences behind which we lived. The older I became, the more this Germany took on the contours of a man, a German man who would love me, love what was female in me. After all, if you excluded what was Russian in me, there was no reason why the rest of me might not be quite acceptable, perhaps even desirable. My femaleness had become my only hope, and in the darkness where this story began, I can see myself climbing up one of the clothes poles at the back of the "houses". It must have been about the same time as my first trip to the hairdresser's, when my lice were discovered. Sliding down the pole was one of the little things I liked to do when there was nobody around to play with – climbing up, whizzing down, climbing up, whizzing down, until the whole thing got boring. And it was on one such occasion that I noticed it for the first time. I was holding on right at the top of the pole as usual, enjoying the feeling of anticipation before letting go, and then just as I was beginning to slide, I suddenly fell off the pole backwards and landed in the grass. I lay there stunned, unable to comprehend what had happened to me. I still had the sliding feeling of the pole between my thighs. The secret pleasure this gave me had always been one of my reasons for sliding down in the first place. But this time it was as if something deep inside me had torn. Something had broken. Something indescribable had shot out of the pole and thrown me to the ground. I lay there in a state of utter terror, quite sure I was mortally ill. My body had suddenly become foreign to me. I couldn't understand what was happening to it. Something monstrous and name-less had entered it, and whatever it was, this thing had taken up its abode in the darkest and most disreputable region of my body, the place where my illness was coming from, the place that contained the small, secret pleasure which I had constantly nourished, and which had now turned into a monster. During the next few days, I hung around the sinister clothes pole trying to work it out. It had developed a magnetic attraction for me, and nothing felt quite as dangerous as it had done originally. After all, nobody knew anything about my illness. There were no further symptoms, no pain, no terrible skin disease. In fact, there was something about this illness I really quite liked. At night, when I was alone in the dark secrecy of my bed, I investigated the origin and substance of this illness. I searched for proof of its presence in me, and found it. I began to want this illness. It began to want me. It wouldn't let me go. I knew something forbidden had me in its grip, something nameless that would be my undoing, something I was powerless to resist. But it was not until after my arrival at the convent that I realised what really was the matter with me. For my situation was much worse than I could possibly have imagined. It was a mortal sin I was committing, the mortal sin of unchastity. It was the Devil that had taken up his abode in me. I had passed through the gateway to hell, inside me ever since I was born. I was not Christ's bride, but the bride of the Devil himself. I was one of Satan's brood who had got inside the sacred walls of the convent. And all the remedies recommended to us as the weapons of our daily fight against this lurking depravity – prayer, fasting, thirsting, self-sacrifice, taking vows, praying again, to the Holy virgin, to St. Anthony – not only failed to cure me, but they seemed to have the opposite effect from that intended. The more violently I resisted it, the more my illness flourished. Indeed, my attempts to combat it merely seemed to attract the Devil's attention. The only thing left for me was to inflict upon myself the punishments I knew I deserved. At night, as soon as it was dark and quiet in the dormitory, I subjected myself to a series of harrowing scientific experiments. I sacrificed my body to the dictates of higher necessity, to the imperatives of cold, unfeeling machines that tested my obedience and willingness to endure suffering. I was an object which could not be held guilty for the pleasure that I felt. I had no will of my own, an object who was in total submission to the power of machines. I was being forced to feel pleasure, damned to feel pleasure. And I began to feel more and more pleasure in pain itself. I was not to know at that stage that my sufferings had only just begun, that they were still mercifully shrouded in the veil of darkness. But my ignorance was not to last. It wasn't long before I was kneeling in the cathedral, in a dark chamber called a confessional, where I was supposed to confess everything to an invisible German priest behind a latticed screen. How often? In words? In thoughts? In deeds? Alone or with others? And in accepting absolution, I was wedded to the Devil for ever. For I had confessed to nothing. Nothing! And the following day was the day of my first Communion, the day *I* was supposed to enter the holy community of the convent! Instead, I desecrated the body of Christ. And I continued to do so with each new day I remained at the convent. And I failed to confess to it every following Saturday. My sacrilege thus took on such astronomical proportions that even hell seemed a place of mercy by comparison with what I must deserve. But what did that matter in the end! I wasn't interested in what happened to me after my death. Even before coming to the convent, I had only survived by going underground, by keeping my real identity a secret. The only reason I was alive at all was because nobody knew anything about me, because I had managed to delude everyone into thinking I was someone else. The figure which I presented to the outside world was a product of my imagination, in total contrast to my real self. I was like a chameleon, changing my camouflage to deceive whichever enemy threatened me. And my desperate desire to be visible was a desire for my imaginary persona to become visible, a figure which adapted itself to each new change in my circumstances, and whose attributes were always those that I felt to be most opportune. And because I still hadn't managed to become identical with this figure, because my biological stigma always succeeded in destroying it, I realised I would have to be even more skilful in my tactics of deception. I would have to work more ruthlessly at destroying myself. It was the only way to defeat my stigma, the only way to deny my true nature.

There was no denying anything to my father following the night I had spent in the coal cellar. When I rang his doorbell for the second time that morning, he opened the door and, for the first time ever, saw me as I really was. He saw me in my forbidden, red, high-heeled shoes. He saw me in my forbidden American taffeta dress. He saw everything in me for which he normally used the word "whore", and although I didn't know what that really meant, I knew it was my father's word for my secret illness, for my iniquity. I was certain he could see not only my school report, not only the German "Linden", but also Achim Uhland. In fact I was sure he could see Achim Uhland more than anything else in me; Achim Uhland, who hadn't rescued me, but had abandoned me to the night. He could see that I'd been reduced to sleeping in a coal cellar, that I'd had no alternative, had nothing to fall back on. He could see that I'd been forced to put myself into his hands. The combination of my gawdy get-up and the dirt from the coal cellar had revealed everything there was to see in me. The sheer obviousness of it all, the fact that I could do nothing but admit to my defeat and impotence and stand there pleading for my father's mercy, seemed to make him more lenient, as if my admission of guilt had finally given him what he wanted. Without saying a word to me, he opened the door to my room. He had an almost contented expression on his face. Then I heard the key turning in the lock behind me. But my mind had stopped working. The only thing I could think of was my camp-bed and Red Cross blankets – warmth!

I was woken by a burning itch. It was a strange sensation, a pain I didn't recognise, and it seemed to be coming from the other end of me under the blankets. I was lying in bed just as I had emerged from the cellar, covered in a layer of black dirt that had now become sodden and oily. The only thing I had taken off was my shoes, and it was from my bare feet that the burning itch was coming. The light in the room told me that it must be midday at least. Perhaps it was already afternoon. The shock of having slept such a long time immediately made me feel wide awake. The flat was utterly quiet. Was my father sitting in the kitchen reading, drinking and smoking as always at this time on Saturday? Or was there something unusual about his stillness? Did it perhaps intimate that there was some incredible trial in store for me? For the first time since I had come back to live with my father, I hadn't had to do the Saturday cleaning, and that in itself was such a major departure from the norms which my father had established that my terror grew with every waking second. I carefully swung my feet out from under the blanket. They were swollen bright red, and my toes, which itched incessantly, shone like frozen cherries. When I stood up it was like walking on broken glass. I crept to the door and, as quietly as I could, pressed down the door handle. Finding it still locked, I felt something akin to relief. For the time being at least, this was all very typical of my father's usual way of treating me when I was a little late home from school. As a punishment for my dawdling, he would lock me in my room and keep me there until the following morning. This time, however, there could be little doubt that I was merely being detained pending a punishment more fitting, and more conclusive. Suddenly, I was overcome by another severe fit of painful coughing. Everything went black. I only just managed to hold myself steady against some piece of furniture. At the same time, the noise of my coughing made me press my other hand to my mouth in dismay. Choking on the wave of nausea that welled up inside me, I remembered I had eaten nothing since the day before yesterday. The two Coca-Colas which Hans had bought me at the "Linden" were all my stomach had had in two days. The five-mark note that I had stolen must still be in my bra. I felt for it, and my fingers found the tiny piece of folded paper, still wrapped in the cotton-wool between my skin and the padded cup of my bra. Naturally my father would have discovered by now that five marks were missing from the drawer. A new wave of terror passed through me. What if he had discovered my school report? What if he had gone looking for it and had found it at the bottom of the wardrobe? With my heart throbbing, I opened the squeaky door of the wardrobe as carefully as I could, pausing to listen for any sound that broke the uncanny silence beyond my bedroom door. My mother's dresses had once hung in this wardrobe and I thought I could smell the scent from a small, dark-blue bottle of French perfume which my father had once brought back for my mother from one of his tours, along with a mouth organ for myself. The smell of my mother, though mingled now with the stale air of the woodworm-ridden wardrobe, was almost shockingly distinct. I hastily bent down to the floor of the wardrobe and lifted up the newspaper. The report was intact, exactly where I had left it under the yellowed pages of Cyrillic print. I had already worked out what I was going to say when my father asked me about my report. But even if he believed me, which seemed unlikely, the very fact of my attempted flight the day before – which, of course, my father had recognised as such, and which would expose the story I had prepared about my report as a lie – was reason enough to keep me under lock and key. This room was bound to be only the first stage of my arrest. There was only one thing to do. I would have to escape through the window before it was too late. A moment later, I had made up my mind. With my heart missing a beat at every sound I made, I packed a bundle of clothes as fast as I could, constantly trying to ignore the unbearable itching of my toes which had now turned bright scarlet and were evidently suffering from frost-bite. As noiselessly as possible, I opened first one, then the other casement of the window and threw my bundle out onto the grass. Luckily for me, the clothes lines at the back were empty, which meant there was nobody in the laundry. On the other hand, it could also mean that the outside door of the laundry was locked. Taking my chance, I climbed down after my bundle, the last drop to the ground sending a searing pain through my feet. My father's bedroom looked out onto the laundry garden next to mine, and there was an ugly piece of material drawn across his window, which I had to polish every Saturday. For a moment I was sure I had seen the material move slightly. I grabbed my bundle, which contained my second-best dress, my red high-heeled shoes as before, a comb, fresh underwear and an old nightdress instead of a towel, and hurried down the outside steps to the laundry. Because the neighbours had disregarded the German house rules, the door had been left unlocked, and I entered the crypt-like semi-darkness, shivering at the memory of how cold it had been the night before. Only a few days had passed since I was in here last, boiling the washing in the giant iron tank in the corner, pressing and then rubbing the clothes on the ribbed wooden board. I took a secret pleasure in this activity, for it allowed me to identify with the toils of womanhood, and my aching back, my burning shoulders and chafed knuckles were a small price to pay for the sweet sensation of adulthood. But the ritual that preceded these strenuous exertions devastated me every time. I had to stand in my father's bedroom and watch while he sorted out the dirty washing into things that had to be boiled and things that shouldn't be boiled. I was supposed to watch as his pupil, just like when he lit the stove for his bath. And what my father was really demonstrating was his immeasurable power over me, and my immeasurable impotence in the face of that power. I watched his finely-sculpted salmon-pink hands. He had a long, manicured finger nail on the little finger of his right hand, which he called his "tool". I watched him pick up my dirty underwear piece by piece and subject it to intensive scrutiny. He investigated every centimetre of it, and it felt to me as if he were exploring every centimetre of my body. Filled with dismay, burning with the shame of it, I stood there and watched it happen, watched my father fingering my dirt, touching all of me, possessing me totally. The pieces of underwear did nothing to resist him; through them, I was at my father's mercy. I was naked. I was completely helpless. I was a piece of underwear in his hands.

I had the unbelievable good fortune to find a small piece of soap on the laundry floor. Straining my ears to the jumble of distant sounds that came now and then from inside the house, I quickly got out of my coal-black clothes. The jet of icy water from the hose took away my breath, shocking my skin with the glacial temperatures of the previous night. My soapy hands trembled as I hurried to rub the stubborn, oily blackness out of my body and hair. Oddly, the cold immediately soothed the burning itch in my feet. I could hardly believe the sight of my clean, bright skin. I hastily dried myself and slipped into my tight green dress with its black woollen fringe just below the hip. Now I was the girl again that Achim Uhland had kissed after our wind-blown ride on his moped. I forced my numbed feet back into the red high-heels, and using the dark glass of the laundry door as a mirror, back-combed my wet hair as best I could. I then tucked the five-mark note back into my bra, stuffed the clothes that I'd worn in the cellar the night before into the stove of the boiler and left the laundry.

As always, the Capitol cinema marked the border for me where the "houses" ended and the German town began. Now it was also where Achim Uhland began. I stopped for a moment outside the cinema and looked at the stills from the films that were showing. I had seen three films in my life, and each had been an unforgettable experience. One of them was called "Scott's Last Journey", another "It's Growing Dark, Albert Schweitzer"; both of these had been shown in the refectory at convent. But the Capitol was where I had seen my very first film. One day on the way home from school, I had found a five-mark piece lying on the street. Five marks was a fortune to me in those days. I had looked down in disbelief at the big, silver coin in my hand, unable to decide what to do with it. I probably had a vague idea of what the money would have meant to my mother, who never knew how she was going to pay her next grocery bill or how she was going to get her shoes repaired. But I kept my find secret, and as soon as I had spooned out the usual plate of cabbage soup, which was called *borsch* on some days and *solyanka* on others, I slipped out into the yard. When I got to the German shop at the "houses", I bought whatever took my fancy: chocolate marshmallows, jaffa cakes, cherry lollies and chocolate waffles. With these treasures under my arm, I crept past the windows of our flat and was soon sitting in the dark in the third tier of the Capitol for the afternoon performance of a film called "Vita mala". For some time afterwards I was unable to decide what had made the deepest impression on me. Was it the prehistoric mountain landscape with its gigantic waterfalls and misty dragons winding their way through bottomless chasms? Was it the murder of the cruel, alcoholic father who had subjected his family to long, inhuman sufferings? Or was it Silvelie with her crown of golden plaits, who had escaped the misery of her childhood and become the wife of a rich, handsome lawyer in town?

It was the first time that I had ever been on the High Street on a Saturday afternoon. I had often dreamt of it during the bleak weekends I spent at home under my father's thumb. The mysterious attraction of the High Street at weekends, when everyone was free and out to enjoy themselves, had always seemed to me to be identical with my secret and desperate longing to meet someone there. The High Street was perhaps the only Street where I could find Achim Uhland, or be found by him. Perhaps he had taken it for granted that we would see each other here again today. How was I to know? Didn't everyone meet here? It was certainly true that the High Street was exceptionally crowded. Boys and girls were sauntering up and down the street in their new spring clothes, and although a few shadows were already falling on the street, it was still unusually summery and warm for the time of year, just as it had been in the cemetery the day before. And yet I was still shivering, and my burning cough had started up again. It seemed to be coming from somewhere deep down in my frozen body, from some frozen core that could no longer be warmed. I suddenly felt dizzy and faint again, and all I could think of was the five-mark note and of getting something to eat at last. Having a full stomach, which I had once thought of as normal and had therefore taken for granted, was now a thing of the past, something that seemed lost for ever. The only thing I could take for granted now was what I could purchase for five marks.

But the shops in town were already closed. I would only be able to get something from the shop at the "houses", but I didn't dare go too near my father's. Anxiously, I studied a menu hanging on the wall outside a restaurant. I hardly knew any of the dishes on it. Not many of them cost more than five marks, but the restaurant seemed so refined. Its crown glass windows prevented me from seeing what it was like inside, and there was a golden horn hung above the door, so that I simply felt too shy to go in. Then I thought of the railway station. To begin with, it seemed incredibly far away. It was right at the other side of town, almost as far as the huge grey buildings and chimneys of the factory at the edge of town where my father worked. But I was soon standing at the street-sales counter of the station restaurant, sweating from my exertions and barely able to control my greed as I ordered two pairs of *wienerwurst*. The change was enough to pay for a bar of chocolate and a packet of biscuits, too. I couldn't remember the last time that I'd held such delicious things in my hands, or whether there had even been a last time. But it didn't matter anyway; my hunger was so great, I could hardly taste what I was eating. I stuffed the sausages, biscuits and chocolate into my mouth all at the same time, trembling at the sight of every lost crumb. In my present condition, I should probably have found even my father's peppery, oily Russian soups edible, which he cooked in a big aluminium pot, always making enough to last us several days. He didn't seem to mind when the soup turned sour, or when it formed slimy bubbles on his plate after being warmed up for the third or fourth time. On the contrary, this was how he seemed to like it. I sat opposite him, rigid with horror and disgust, staring down at a plate of what looked like putrefied flesh. And yet this substance seemed to be his very reason for reheating the soup so often. There seemed to be nothing more satisfying to him than to sit there spooning this stuff from his plate with tears in his eyes and sweat pouring down his red face. Slurping and smacking his lips in contentment, he would finally scrape up the pepper that had settled on the bottom of his plate and lean back in his chair puffing and panting and wiping the sweat from his brow with a handkerchief. Then, especially when he had been drinking, he would start praising "our Russian soups" and railing at the Germans, whom he accused of eating grass and wearing spectacles. In particular he inveighed against red-headed Germans, whom he hated bitterly for some reason, and returned again and again to the subject of German soups, his anger increasing every time he mentioned them. He despised German soups, and insulted them with such vigour that it seemed impossible not to conclude that German soups were the source of all his woes, indeed, the root of all evil in the world.

At last, with the food in my stomach weighing heavy like a stone, I was back on the High Street. There was nothing left for me to do now but walk up and down and wait. My feet felt like some shapeless mass that had been squeezed into my shoes. They had started to burn again, too, and were itching unbearably. It was beginning to get dark again already. There were some boys leaning against the railings at the edge of the market place who whistled at me as I went past. I was embarrassed to have to walk about here alone. People could see that I didn't have anywhere to go and was just waiting. The other boys and girls who passed me, most of whom I recognised, all seemed to be doing what they had set out to do. They were walking up and down the High Street in couples or groups, and that was the whole point of an evening like this. The terrible thing about this small town was that everybody here knew who everybody else was. I couldn't hide the fact that I came from the "houses" at the edge of town. Everybody knew who belonged to that scum and who didn't. Refugees from the East had always stuck out in the town like a sore thumb anyway, since they seemed incapable of leading a normal, middle-class life. I remembered not being allowed into the public swimming baths as a child. I was told that people from the "houses" didn't wash themselves. So even then, everybody had known who I was.

It was already the second or third time I had wandered up and down the High Street. Like everyone else, I was sauntering back and forth between the market place and Parade Square. "The German Linden" seemed closed this evening. Nothing stirred behind the darkening foliage of the huge lime tree which hid the building almost totally with its leaves. This evening everything was centred on the balustrades at the edge of the market square. The boys usually sat there perched on the iron railings, or stood leaning against them as if they were looking over a ship's rails, calling to the girls who came strolling by, or wolf-whistling after them. I had already bumped into one or two boys and girls from my class at school, and their knowing looks had filled me with an excruciating shame. They made me feel as weird as I looked, and I stuck out a mile here, on their home ground. Their withering looks brought out the full extent of my humiliation. This High Street was all that I had left. Achim Uhland was my only hope. I was reduced to begging for mercy.

Those who spoke to me at all at school called me "Russla", or "Russian bitch". They laughed raucously at me and asked me whether it were really true that we washed our potatoes in the lavatory pan, or whether "Russian bitches" really didn't wear any knickers. Sometimes, they called me a "slut", and I felt that was exactly what their looks were transmitting to me as we passed each other on the High Street. I could never remember when I first heard certain words. They had somehow always been there. They felt like a part of me, like my skin. "Russian swine" was another of these words. I first came across it when I was about eight or nine and was having a fight with a German boy on the school playground and had hit him in the genitals. Was that really when it first was? The words "Russian swine" scrawled on the blackboard in white chalk? Perhaps it was long before that. Perhaps I had first heard these words holding my mother's hand. She was silent and we were wearing our refugees' rags, walking down a street that was no more than the debris left by a war. Perhaps the word had stuck to me then, though it was meant for my mother. Or it was in the air we breathed, and had come to mean me long before my memory began. It had come to mean me and my mother at a time when I was one body with her, one body with a young, Ukrainian forced-labour convict who had got pregnant on some dirty camp-bed and who stood at a lathe with me in her belly, making shells in a Leipzig arms factory. It had stuck to us on the street where people knew who she was because of the numbers forced-labour convicts had to wear on their clothes, like the stars Jews had to wear, except that such convicts were at least allowed to live and make shells in a factory, shells that were used against their own people. And although speaking to enemy aliens was forbidden to the German population, although it was an offence that could end in the death penalty, the prohibition probably didn't extend as far as certain words that could be hurled at labour convicts as they passed on the street.

"Russian swine", "Russian bitch", "slut", "Russian slut" are words from the language in which I'm telling this story. Is that why I so often feel speechless? Or why every word in this story seems false? Maybe language baulks at these terms, which lie between me and everything this story relates. Or is it simply that my own language can't get beyond them because certain German words – certain standard German words, or words in German dialect, German words coupled with the Russian equivalents my father used for me – are indelibly stained on me? How can my language be the language of a country in which speaking to the likes of me was once punishable by death?

At the time, the background to all this was unknown to me. I had heard a lot about Stalin by the time I was sixteen, about the Communists, about all kinds of atrocities and acts of barbarism that had happened in Russia. I had heard that the Russians had attacked Germany and burnt down its cities. I had heard that they had butchered German children and raped German women. But I had never heard the other side of the story. I had never heard of concentration camps, or of lampshades made of human skin. I had never heard of German bombers over the Soviet Union, of Russian towns and villages burnt to the ground, or of "Messerschmidts tearing up the dawn silence like ravens . . ." I had heard nothing of the twenty million the Germans had killed in the Soviet Union. The only bit of it that was left over for me in the provincial Germany of the fifties and sixties were the words "Russian slut". For those who called me such names, these two words really amounted to the same thing: the combination of the Russian and the female in me. Beyond a certain age, I had almost always experienced people's contempt for my origins as something directed against me as a woman, for racial and national hatred always culminate in contempt for the bodies of women who belong to that race or nation. But at the time, all this was unknown to me. I was ignorant of the true story (and perhaps I still am). I was that story myself, and perhaps I still am. It is the story of how my background was unknown to me, and a story in which that may still be the case.

But how tedious the details of this story are! How boringly predictable most of it is! The rest of what happened between myself and Achim Uhland is just too obvious for words . . .

When it was already dark and the vicious jaws of yet another cold night were closing on me fast, I met Hans on the High

Street. He took me to a pub, the "Moonlight", where Achim Uhland was sitting with Manuela Köhler, who was in my class at school. To my eyes, she was also the most attractive girl in the whole town, the one most like the film stars on the posters at the Capitol.

I felt Hans's hand on my back, pushing me through the crush on the small dance floor to the bar. I had promised to let him kiss me if he took me to Achim Uhland, and then I was holding a glass in my hand, hardly noticing what I was drinking. It was a biting liquid that smelled of ammonia and immediately took the edge off things. "Jailhouse Rock" was on the jukebox. The volume was turned up so loud that the tune was almost unrecognisable. Flakes of bright light whirled round and round like snow in the semi-darkness. I kept on catching glimpses of Achim Uhland and Manuela Köhler through the surging bodies on the dance floor. They were sitting on their own at one of the tables at the far end of the room. Achim Uhland had his arm round Manuela's shoulders. She was laughing, and evidently resisting his advances. The image kept disappearing, then flashing back up. It was like looking through the window of a moving train, or through a ship's porthole with wave after wave drowning out the view. Hans had ordered me a second glass of the ammonia-smelling drink and its taste mingled with that of Hans's wet kisses which, in keeping with my promise, I now had to let him give me. His broad, rosy-cheeked face, which reminded me for some strange reason of Christmas tree decorations, or of deep fried pastry, blurred into the snowflakes in front of me. I felt his sweaty hand somewhere, sticking to my body. Then someone came over and asked me to dance. Once again, I saw Achim Uhland and Manuela Köhler through the ship's porthole. They were now entwined in each other's arms among the snowflakes on the dance floor. Then it was back to

Hans and ammonia. Someone offered me a cigarette, and I took it in my fingers just as I had seen Manuela take cigarettes from Achim Uhland, with her long fingers and varnished finger nails. The smoke merged with the taste of the alcohol and Hans's kisses in my mouth, and as soon as it penetrated my lungs, the train in which I'd been sitting plunged off the rails into a dark abyss. I felt as though I were being shaken by a kind of earthquake. I thought I was going to choke to death on the sharp burning feeling inside me, and then – darkness. Later, I couldn't remember what had happened, only that I had suddenly found myself back out on the street, still on Hans's arm, and that the cold night air had sobered me up. I saw Achim Uhland and Manuela on the street, too. They were standing some distance away from us, and they seemed to be having a fight. Manuela was shouting furiously and trying to disentangle herself from Achim Uhland's violent grip. But suddenly he let her go. A tall, elegant young man had appeared from inside, and Manuela immediately disappeared with him into the Karmann Ghia parked in front of the pub. Then I was standing in front of Achim Uhland, having at last managed to get Hans's arm off me. I was standing in front of him and saw something flash in his eyes, something which I immediately recognised before he spoke, something that had been coming to me for a long time: "Why don't you just piss off, you Russian slut!" It was the most boring, the most predictable thing in this story . . .

It was late at night. The contents of my schoolbag lay in a heap on the table in my room.

"Where have you been?" my father asked. He had come from his bed and was wearing underpants and a vest.

"Walking," I answered.

"Where have you been walking?"

"Outside."

"Who were you walking with?"

"No one."

"I see. With no one, eh? . . . And where's your report?"

"Nowhere."

"Where's the money you stole?"

"Nowhere."

"What have you done with it?"

"Nothing."

"What have you done with your report?"

"Nothing. We didn't get our reports."

"You're lying."

"No."

"You are lying."

"No, I'm not. They're not giving us reports till the end of the school year."

"You're lying. Where have you been?"

"Nowhere."

"Take those shoes off at once – and that dress."

"No."

My father hit me, on the head as usual. He held me firmly with one hand while bringing the other down on me like an axe. Outwardly his behaviour was entirely unemotional. It was mechanical, as if he were chopping wood, and as if he were now having to deal with a piece that was particularly hard and intransigent. He drew back his arm as far as he could before each blow, leaving a short, merciful pause before his fist came crashing down on me again with renewed, cold-blooded vigour. I crossed my arms over my head. They were my only protection. Not against the pain, since I didn't feel pain while he was actually hitting me, but against the force and sound of these blows. The first was enough to frighten me out of my wits. Under its impact, my head seemed to split into a thousand flying pieces. And each further blow was like a shell exploding in the echo of the last, so that the echo grew louder and louder. But can words really describe something like this? By using his fist, my father had broken down a barrier. On the other side of that barrier there are no holds barred. What this means is that, from the first blow onwards, the only thing you can be sure of is this: "Anything can happen to me now." You are utterly helpless before the infinitely superior strength of the other. Your body has lost any right it once had to its own territory. Even your skin is not your own, since the other, with his superior strength, can overpower it, take it away, or destroy it whenever he wants. You are nothing, a helpless body in someone else's hands, nothing more, nothing less. And you begin to hate your own body. Because it is through your body that you experience how miserably weak you are, how totally powerless. The stronger person has thus achieved what he set out to do. You are now in full agreement with him. What you are saying is, "You are better than me because you are stronger; I am worse than you because I am weaker. I am worthless, pitiful, worthy only of your hatred. You are quite right to beat me."

These beatings were the only bodily contact between my father and me. Beating me was, after all, a form of bodily contact. He was touching me in a manner he considered to be legitimate for a father. It was only the fact that he hit me exclusively on the head that showed how frightened he was of the rest of my body. I didn't let out a sound while his blows rained down on me. The cold, almost technical nature of this bodily contact was my only real protection. I played dead. I didn't react at all. And because I showed no reaction, because my body refused to submit to him even under this torture, his blows became more and more furious. He wanted me to love him, to hate him, to fear him. He wanted me to show him that he was hurting me, wounding me, that he knew how to wound me. I refused to show him anything, and eventually he let me go.

A few minutes later he came back to my room with a hammer. I thought he was going to kill me. Instead he went over to the window and started hammering nails into the window frame (thirteen of them as I later discovered). Then he brought a bucket and a jug of water and locked me in.

One of my earliest memories is of a corridor. This corridor was in a former Nazi barracks. We were staying there in a room that was packed with refugees. We had been waiting for weeks, maybe months, for exit permits to go to America. I can see suitcases, grey coats, yellow faces behind curtains of tobacco smoke. It is winter. Christmas. I'm three or four and my pneumonia is a rabbit with red eyes and black fur. It's hot and just sits there on my chest in the dark and won't move. Somewhere deep inside me there is a safe place called America. But my breathing can't reach it because the rabbit's on my chest and won't let my breath through. The rabbit is crushing me, suffocating me. And suddenly I'm running down a corridor. It's high and narrow and has very bright lights, and I'm wheezing and whining and screaming for my mother but I can't find her. I'm running, and I'm all alone with the rabbit. And my mother can drive the rabbit off my chest with her magic green cream, but my mother's gone away and perhaps she's gone to America and has left me alone with the rabbit who wants to crush me. I'm running because I've got to get to America. And I run through a tunnel with no air, through glaring, tired, unchanging light. I've only got a short nightie on and I'm running in bare feet through the icy light that showers sleet over me. I'm running but I never get there, never reach America, never get to my mother. And I can see myself running through the narrowest point just as I'm about to suffocate, through the eye of the needle, running, running...

A room with four stone walls, a camp bed and wooden shelves painted Prussian blue . . . And I'm running, running through a tunnel, through the eye of the needle, through a nightmare that won't end . . .

How long have I been locked up in here? I count the first, second, third day. Then I lose count. At first I feel almost glad to be alone in my room. When I wake up in the morning I can still hear the echo of the blows in my head. The bucket is my toilet. The jug of water . . . I'm going to be in here a long time. I see that right away.

At first I try to open the window. I pull at the casements but the window is like a wall. Even the scissors I use as pliers, as a lever, are powerless against the rusty nails in the wooden frame.

At first, the sound of my father's feet coming down the corridor frightens me. As though I'm going to be taken to my execution. But then gradually it dawns on me. My execution is already happening in this room.

Neither my hunger, nor my cough, nor my frozen toes itching incessantly under the warm blankets – nothing could be as bad as this thirst. Stupidly, but also because I was so hungry, I drank all my water on the first day. It tasted of milk, of that indescribably delicious drink that milk turned into when I was allowed to fetch it from the dairy. I would walk all alone through the mystery of the evening in the German town, and the milk would taste of this mystery. There was a mystery in all things, a mystery that cast a magic spell over me, a mystery I called "German". It was the milky smell of those evenings I tasted in the water from the jug.

At first I hope the neighbours will help me. When I hear the outer door slam and I'm quite sure my father has gone to work, I bang on the wall of Marjanka's flat. I stand on a chair and bang on the ceiling with a clothes-hanger so that the Serbs can hear me. I shout. I drum on the wall. I know they can hear me because I can hear them too through the thin walls, but no one answers me. Just as no one answers the Serb woman when she screams in mortal terror every Saturday; just as no one helps Marjanka when she runs across the yard on her dropsied legs, trying to escape from the Romanian with the wooden leg.

Exhausted, I fall asleep. I dream. I dream I have an iron head that I keep ramming full tilt against a wall. I have to keep on doing this until the wall gives way. My life depends on it. But the forces are evenly balanced. I don't stand a chance. My head is made of iron. The wall is made of stone. The iron has just as little chance against the stone as the stone against the iron. It will carry on like this for ever, iron against stone, stone against iron. I'll never be able to break down the wall, and the wall will never smash my head. But what really astonishes me is the sensitivity of my iron head. When I bang it against the wall, it hurts just as much as an ordinary head of flesh and blood. Someone ought to be told this. Someone should be informed that iron can hurt itself. But I'm the only one who knows. That's the horrible thing about this dream. Nobody knows except me. I'm all alone with the strange secret of my iron head, with the strange secret of a material that's sore and doesn't stand a chance – me.

I come up for air and sink again. Is this sleep? A wild dream? Hallucination? I don't know. I've got no saliva left. There's a brassy ringing reverberating in my head. My bowels are on fire. Covering the bucket I'm supposed to use as a toilet with newspapers hasn't helped; there's an obnoxious stench in the room. The air is bitter and sharp. My heart is racing, my lungs panting. My body seems to be craving the liquid it has lost, and the thicker the stench, the greater the craving. I am suffocating on myself, on the fumes of my own sewage, on the vicious circle that my body has become.

I keep on returning to the window and tearing at the frame while I still have the strength. I drum my fists on the walls. And eventually, I start beating on the door. I call to my father. I plead with him. I beg for mercy. I have surrendered. My resistance is broken: "Papa". All I can do is whimper through the door: "Papa, open the door!" But soon I no longer have the energy to whimper and weakness crashes over me in great waves that seem to be washing everything away, until even my burning thirst disappears and a green lichen covers my eyelids. At last the water takes me, the river, and I fall, a part of the great ringing flood, with no pain.

For years, I had kept the piece of paper folded in a compartment of my purse. I knew the Moscow address on it by heart. There was a district, a street name, a house number and the number of a flat, but no name. That was the strange thing about it – there was no name. And also I'd found it in my father's laundry book and not in his address book. That didn't necessarily mean much, of course. The address probably had something vaguely to do with the Russian newspapers and magazines my father had sent to him from all kinds of distant places. It had probably got into his laundry book by accident. But that made it even odder that there was no name. What was more, it was evidently the address of someone's flat in Moscow. Could it be that my father maintained some sort of contact with his past, with old acquaintances, or even perhaps with relatives in the Soviet Union? It seemed unlikely to me. In fact, it was unthinkable. My father's past didn't exist. His existence had begun in Germany as a homeless Russian. Before that, there had been next to nothing. He had never been a normal social being with relations, acquaintances and friends. He had never had any connection with the world around him. It was only later when he got old and frail that he would sometimes talk about his childhood by the Volga. Or rather, he talked about the Volga itself, about its colossal size, its length and breadth and depth, about ships, markets and Easter festivities, about various incidents, great and small, in a world which could not have been more remote, and yet which still managed to make my father's fading eyes light up as if nothing had changed. This world seemed to break off abruptly with the death of both his parents. At least, my father's own story broke off abruptly with the death of his parents, both of whom had died of typhus during the famine shortly after the Revolution. After that, there was only the story of how he had been the oldest of four brothers and had managed to bring his three younger brothers through the years of famine. Hardly more than a child, he had had to sell his parents' house for a sack of flour in order to stay alive. But then everything came to a standstill – his brothers, the Volga, his country, even my father himself. The older he got, the more often his story would come full circle to the place it had begun, to the Volga, the ships, the markets, Easter festivities, harmless incidents. It was like the hands of a clock passing the twelve. The story would go right up to the Revolution, then through it, so that the Revolution itself wasn't included; and it would go right up to his parents' death, but the death itself wouldn't be included. It passed through them without getting to them, as it were, and thus returned to its point of departure, the Volga. The Volga was his place of origin all right. That was clear by now. But after that there was nothing, or certainly nothing that could be described as a vital relationship between my father and today's Soviet Union.

When he stumped out of his room to go to the toilet, out into the corridor of the old people's home, feeling his way forward clumsily with his stick, like a child clutching his mother's hand and attempting to walk for the first time, I hastily wrote down the address. It felt like stealing, or like entering forbidden territory. I stuffed the piece of paper into my purse.

The years went by and soon I had my own connections in Moscow, people with names, faces and voices, different areas of town, streets I would walk down as though in a dream world, surrounded by an aroma I wanted to call home but couldn't, because it refused to be breathed in. And even if proof of my true origins did exist, even if the piece of paper in my purse were such a proof, what good would it do me? What would it change? I didn't want that change anyway. I didn't want any origins, or proof. I especially didn't want proof that I was my father's daughter.

The name of the district on my piece of paper did not conjure up a residential area in Moscow to me. It was more reminiscent of an old Russian village somewhere in the taiga, or even on the banks of the Volga. It wasn't the town but the countryside one heard in the word, not the present but the past. It was a long way from the centre, so Nadya had told me, right on the edge of Moscow. That was all she knew about it.

What I found when I got there was a modern, sterile housing estate. Perhaps there had been cottages there once; one often saw the remains of poor, dilapidated, sleepy villages on the outskirts of town. But now there were concrete apartment blocks rising into the stifling August sky which hung over the town like a spongy mass, saturated with poisonous fumes and the brimstony smell of burning. It was one of those typical areas of tower blocks in the suburbs, where one tends to feel simply forlorn. Of course the street name I had given the taxi driver no longer existed. Absurdly, the name of the district was the sole remaining vestige of the place that had once existed there, and it now denoted its opposite. It was quite obvious that the address dated from before my father's emigration. And even if there had been a connection to some hidden part of my father's past, then that past had been stamped into the ground long ago, for between then and now lay the chaos and destruction of a war. Then and now were separated by famines, mass arrests, mass deportations and mass executions, by the strokes of fate of a whole lifetime, indeed of an entire historical epoch. But I was probably right in the first place, and the whole thing was a mistake of some kind, just a muddled note of my father's with no significance whatsoever.

But Nadya disregarded all this with the same, unswerving determination that led her to defy anything apparently futile. In no time at all, she had asked half a dozen passers-by, had spoken to the old women on the benches between the giant tower blocks, sitting there as though between the garden huts on their allotments. Eventually, she found out that the street we were looking for had only recently changed its name. It had been given a name that was better suited to the area, a name that echoed the heroic fanfare of progress. I struggled to grasp what this meant. The old women had said only recently; the street name had only recently changed. That meant the street whose name I had found in my father's laundry book had existed here a short time ago in this modern Moscow moonscape. How had my father come by a Moscow address dating from a time after his emigration, an address in contemporary Moscow? Had I really lit upon some secret connection between my father and this Moscow?

Nadya thought we might as well see whether the numbers of the house and flat on our piece of paper corresponded to numbers in the newly named street. The old women sitting on their benches told us how to get there. The street with the new name turned out to be right on the edge of the housing estate. We came to a courtyard with trees and grass, framed by four slightly less modern, but equally gigantic apartment blocks. Obviously, this was where the socialist proletariat lived, huddled together in their futuristic barracks, blessed with baths and central heating. The type of people who lived here considered themselves lucky. The aura of the old village shacks had entered the cramped living space of these buildings along with their new residents. These were the invisible Soviet people, the Soviet masses whose uniform appearance made them look like a herd of pack animals, or like a landslide of grey rocks rolling slowly down the streets. This was where the normal people lived, a people who were simple, heroic and much-praised, the free and happy people of the Soviet Union, a people no one had ever seen, a people who existed only on paper, only in propaganda printed by newspapers which nobody read, in ideological manuals which nobody bought, or on red banners which nobody noticed. Here was the home of the happy people of a workers' and peasants' state that could not have been more distant from the peasants and workers. The happy people of the Soviet Union – a theory that hadn't been put into practice. Could there really be some connection between myself and these people? Was this the people my father had once belonged to? Had he also been part of this grey landslide rolling from street to street? Was there someone living behind these Babylonian rows of windows with whom my father had remained in contact from his room and balcony in a German old people's home, at least until relatively recently? There was something about the place that reminded me of the "houses". It was like a modern, mass produced version of the "houses", a whole city of "houses" that was out of sight and mind of the Soviet metropolis, and which had shot up here to house the lowest strata of Soviet classless society. The thought of someone actually living here to whom I was possibly related, and who would therefore be my only relative beside my parents, immediately brought back my old feelings of shame. But this time it was a shame I felt before the Russian writers who were my friends in Moscow, and before Nadya, who was walking along beside me. Nadya, who belonged to the Moscow intelligentsia, could play Schubert on the piano and knew more about German literature than I did. Until now I had managed to hide – from myself as well as from others – behind the mythical status of a person with no past. But perhaps this was my moment of truth! For the first time in my life, I would be thoroughly visible, exposed for all to see. I felt an intense reluctance towards continuing the search, and a strong desire to take to my heels. I felt ashamed of my reluctance, and ashamed of my own shame about possibly belonging to the miserable, marginalised masses of the Russian proletariat.

The fact that the number I had found in my father's laundry book also existed in the newly named street didn't exactly prove much. Just another No 169! Nor was it particularly significant that there was a flat number 43 in this house. That just meant there was a flat No 3 on the fourth floor. Hardly unusual! There were no names on doors in Moscow. Everything worked on the basis of numbers. So all we could do was ring at this strange door and see what happened. Nadya had already pressed the bell. The glass pupil of the peep-hole stared at us through the grey, varnished door. But what on earth was I going to say if someone opened it? I hadn't even bothered to think about that! I suddenly felt my legs turn to jelly. I could hear my heart pounding somewhere in the silent emptiness of the stairwell. It was as though something awful about me were going to be revealed; as though everything I had ever feared lay beyond this door. Nadya rang again, and a third time. No one came to the door. She tried ringing at one of the other doors. Then at a third door. She tried all five doors on that floor. Nothing. There was nobody about. Upstairs, downstairs – a deathly hush. How could there be nobody at home on the entire fourth floor of a large apartment block at six o'clock in the evening? Did nobody live here at all? Or did the people here live life according to a completely different set of rules? It all seemed quite unreal to me. Was I dreaming? After all – the grey varnished doors with nobody behind them, the stairwell stinking of rotting rubbish, the old women sitting on their benches between the skyscrapers, the puzzle of the street names and numbers . . .? On our way downstairs, we decided to make a last attempt. We rang at a door on the third floor. We heard a scraping noise as though someone we could not see were dragging something towards us across the floor of the flat on the other side of the door. The spastic figure of a woman appeared, panting heavily from the exertion of walking. She had permed hair that was unnaturally black and shone like glass wool. The upper part of her body was at such an extreme angle to her lower half that it was only with great difficulty that she was able to stand up at all, on short, swollen legs. She propped herself up stiffly on the door frame. This woman, an invalid, appeared to be the only living person in the whole house. The journey we had forced her to make to the door had probably been torture to her. I heard Nadya talking, and suddenly heard the woman say my maiden name. It wasn't me she meant, but the people who lived at No 43. "Pure chance!" I thought. "A totally weird coincidence!" The figure of the woman in front of me went blurred. She appeared to be getting closer then further away again, as if through a zoom lens. And then I was standing next to Nadya in a room that resembled a fifties' German sitting room. I saw Nadya tuck a loose strand back into her greyish-brown hair with a graceful movement of her hand, while the woman, supporting herself with one hand on an armchair, was pointing out of the window: "Can you see her? Katya's sitting over there on the steps of the clinic. She's a warder there. Do you see her now?" From this distance, Katya appeared to be one of those ubiquitous little old Russian ladies like the ones we had seen sitting outside between the tower blocks. They were always small, these women, always decrepit, and strangely ageless. For although they weren't all old in reality, they all looked very old. They wore drab overalls, which they put on over their coats in winter, and headscarfs which they even kept on in summer so that one came to think of them as natural extensions of their heads. You saw them everywhere sweeping the pavements, their crooked backs bent over their short birch brooms. They swept the long streets, the large squares, the small squares, the department stores, the theatres and the stations. Everywhere in Moscow there were little old women with brooms, sweeping the great, capital city of the Soviet Union. They were like birds who made their nests in buildings. They were lift attendants and lavatory attendants. They were the so-called custodians of all kinds of indefinable realms, settling in cold niches, keeping themselves warm in winter with felt boots, or if they were lucky, with the last intact filaments of electric fires. You could see them selling their few handfuls of mushrooms in the Moscow markets, arranging them on handkerchiefs which they spread on the ground. Or they sold thin bunches of asters and lilies in stations and cemeteries. They knelt on the stone floors of the last "working" churches, as people called them; the last worshippers in the twilight of a decaying Byzantine splendour. And when I looked at these old women, it was also their fallen husbands and sons I saw. I saw their sisters and daughters, who had been shot, or worked to death in the camps. I saw their old villages and huts. I saw the Volga, the markets, the Easter festivities. I saw the Revolution, although all I saw of it was some distant, chaotic inferno. I saw typhus and hunger. I saw a house sold for a sack of flour. I saw the war, of which I also saw little more than a distant inferno. Nothing in Moscow was more revealing, nothing told me more about Russia than the faces of these old women. Russia was engraved in their faces as though in the rotting bark of old trees. And now one of these little old women had my family name and was somehow related to me.

Perhaps she had seen us arrive and had watched us from her position in the shadows on the steps of the outpatients clinic opposite her house. Nadya's appearance made her conspicuous in this part of town, and the Muscovites, who immediately recognised anything Western, would have picked me out wherever I went. It was a difference they recognised. And this difference did not merely consist in clothing or hairstyles, in more modern spectacles or more sophisticated dentures. Nor could it be reduced to language or behaviour. There was something indefinable that went beyond all these things, like something created by a different metabolism or by a different balance of vitamins. It was immediately visible. Perhaps she had seen us entering her house, and now that we had re-emerged and were heading straight across the courtyard in her direction, perhaps she knew we were looking for her. Here were two strange, rather conspicuous women who she had never seen before, and they were looking for her. Perhaps we were officials of some kind, sent by the authorities to sound her out, to inform on her, to spy on her. Whoever we were, we were utterly foreign in this area, an unknown quantity and therefore not to be trusted. Or perhaps when she finally saw me standing in front of her, my Western appearance aroused a vague suspicion in her, a dark memory of something that terrified her.

What I saw when I got up close to her was a small, haggard woman whose eyes expressed the characteristic indifference of Moscow public service workers. She was wearing white nylon overalls and a white head scarf over grey hair that had been ruined by too many bad perms. She had strikingly blue eyes and a smooth, pale face that seemed cut from the same nylon as her overalls, and in which a fine network of tiny violet veins stood out against the sickly glow of her cheeks. She was a careworn old woman with glassy features who probably had a heart condition, the doorkeeper at an outpatients clinic, a pensioner earning something on the side who lived in one of the anonymous honeycomb structures of a ghostly satellite town on the outskirts of Moscow.

As it turned out, she was my father's sister-in-law, the wife of one of his three brothers. But there was also a barrier between us, a barrier that could be traced back to a Russian tradition. Often, a whole family would be held liable for the crimes of one of its members. Between us stood the fear that she probably felt for her children and grandchildren. It was dangerous to be related to the daughter of a man who had betrayed his country, the daughter of a man who had collaborated with the Germans and who probably still had the death sentence hanging over his head. Between us stood a fear which affected even those whose relatives had moved to the West legally, a fear felt even by my own friends in Moscow, who were privileged and protected by their education and status in society. This fear was prior to the fact, as it were. It was already there long before there was any real reason to feel it. It had its roots in the Stalin era. It was a conditioned reflex, a code that had stamped itself firmly and indelibly upon the nervous system of a whole generation. It was a fear I had attacked in others, a fear that had driven me to distraction. And now this fear had finally reached me, the fear of harming other people by entering into a relationship with them. At the same time, I feared putting myself at risk by attempting to find out the truth about these relationships. Perhaps the only thing that had protected us up until now was the fact that we had had nothing to do with each other, the fact that the two ends of our broken thread had never come together. Perhaps what I was doing now was naive, dangerous, irresponsible. I could hardly blame this woman, my aunt, for showing no sign of joy at my presence. She even avoided eye contact with me, as though to have my image on her retina would already be asking for trouble. But I understood that. What I couldn't understand was why my father had kept this harmless woman secret from me, along with his brother. At least I had now established that his brother was still alive. He had gone off on his bicycle to a nearby laundry. Why were these relations of his such a secret? Why was his need to keep them from me so great that he had kept their address hidden in a laundry book at the old people's home? Even there, he had been careful not to record any names. From the little my aunt had said, I gathered my father and her husband wrote to each other now and then, or at least had done so in the past.

Two days later, I was standing again in front of the grey, varnished door on the fourth floor of tower block No 169, but this time without Nadya. The man who opened the door to me was wearing a bright green shirt and old-fashioned, dark-rimmed spectacles. In fact, he looked quite dapper. The furrows and folds in his gaunt face gave him the air of an owl or a Great Dane, and his resemblance to my father shocked me. My initial reaction was to flinch. He was immediately my enemy, although I quickly saw that there was something likeable in his face, something that betrayed what was possibly a dry sense of humour, a humour as bitter as the taste of sloes. But my first glance had registered only my father, and I had instinctively recoiled from him, recognising an enemy. At the same time, I could feel my image of my father begin to change, too. He had suddenly become a brother, the brother of a man who lived in a tower block in Moscow and who was married to someone called Katya. And since he was the brother of my uncle, that also made him a father; and since I was now a niece, that also made me a daughter. So here I was, holding a ridiculous bottle of Crimean sparkling wine which I had bought at a foreign currency shop. At the same time, my bowels were staging a riot. For almost the whole of the previous hour, during a taxi ride through half Moscow, I had felt as if I were having simultaneous attacks of typhus and dysentery. I don't think I had ever longed to arrive at a place quite so desperately as at the strange flat of an uncle who was a stranger to me. My only possible chance of avoiding imminent disaster had been to confess to this most basic of human needs the moment my uncle opened the door. And before my eyes finally came to rest on the polished tiles of a tiny bathroom, I was taken aback by the sight of a portrait decorated with a bunch of plastic flowers, which hung in the hall against a background of garish, patterned wallpaper. It was a portrait of Josef Vissarionovich Stalin. But surely this couldn't be the answer to all my questions? How could this explain my father's whole past and present?

My uncle hadn't realised I had never known anything about him. He also seemed quite astonished that my father knew nothing of my visit. We sat down to a small, neatly laid table. On it, there was a pan of roast potatoes, a small plate of sliced salami, a bowl of blue plums, a dark loaf and a bottle of vodka. I could only guess at the effort that must have gone into acquiring the salami and plums, standing in two different queues at shops or street kiosks. There was little doubt these had been bought especially for me. My uncle had known I was coming. He had phoned me himself, at Nadya's number, which I had almost had to force his wife to take from me. She herself was nowhere to be seen, and the fact that she seemed to have taken flight as soon as she'd laid the table made me feel all the more uneasy. The small room we were sitting in was evidently the only room in the flat. Its tidiness reminded me of my father's own scrupulous attention to order and cleanliness. It was reminiscent of the obsessive perfectionism of a German sitting room, which, considering there were two elderly people living here in a single room, was a doubly admirable feat. There was only a single, narrow bed standing in one corner of the room. It was too small for anything else, and the painstaking tidiness of the room seemed to me to derive from a sense of shame at the humiliating narrowness of their living conditions. On top of the television in one of the other corners was a standard bust of Lenin, the type of bust one finds in almost every department store in Moscow. Together with the portrait of Stalin, however, which hung in the hall and was immediately visible to anyone entering the flat, the bust lost its typical, popular flavour. It was no longer an irrelevant piece of mass ideological kitsch. It was a threat.

My uncle poured me a glass of vodka. "They've never done anything to us," he said in a strangely reticent, embarrassed tone, as if he felt he had to apologise for something. "On the contrary," he added, "they've given us this flat." Whom did he mean by "they"? My friends used "they" to refer to the invisible, ever-vigilant eye of the State. "They" was a codename for the enemy. But since "they" were so obviously visible here, why should "they" want to do anything to my uncle and his wife who, in spite of everything, seemed to regard this flat as a luxury, as an honour? Was it because they were related to my father, to a traitor, a collaborator? Were "they", or rather their portraits, in this flat to protect my uncle and aunt from the dangers of this kinship? "You know what I mean," my uncle continued, "there was that other business. You know – that story about your father." The astonishment I saw in my uncle's face was evidently the reflection of my own. "You mean your father has never told you?" Who was this man my uncle was talking about? Who was this man my uncle apparently took to be a completely normal human being, the completely normal father of a daughter who knew who her father was? What had come between the man my uncle had known and the man I knew? What was this "other business", this "story" about my father, of which I was naturally just as ignorant as I was about everything else in my father's life? Was there some explanation to be found here? A concrete explanation for my father's flight to Germany? Did this explain the secrecy surrounding the address? Had he kept it hidden to prevent me finding out something he didn't want me to know? Was this the reason why my father had kept his entire past a secret? But my uncle shook his head: "No, I'm afraid I can't tell you anything your father hasn't told you himself." Did my uncle realise that if he stuck to that principle, he couldn't tell me anything at all? He couldn't tell me that a second uncle had died three years previously of a heart attack, or that a third uncle had been one of the officers Stalin had shot for some unexplained reason after the victory over Hitler's Germany. My uncle couldn't say anything that left even the shadow of a mark on the blank page my father was to me – a man who had always kept the dark secret of his life shrouded in silence, concealed behind brute force. This was a man my uncle seemed not to know. Perhaps my father had only become this man when he reached Germany. And perhaps this "other business", this "story" of which I was evidently to remain ignorant, was central to his silence, was its very heart.

My uncle had pronounced the word "Stalin" with particular care, his eyes automatically flicking to the door as he did so. Was he afraid the portrait outside had ears? And if he was afraid of it, why was it hanging there? Was my uncle such a political ignoramus that he didn't realise the days of statutory idolatory were over? And how could he say that "they" had never done anything to him, since they had put his own brother up in front of a firing squad? Quite apart from the fact that shutting two old people up in a single room of not more than fifteen square metres was itself tantamount to a death sentence. Did the pedantic tidiness of this room have something to do with the mentality of an era that had not stopped short of the purges, an era that had possibly also formed my father? Or was this place ruled by the powers of darkness, by the age-old Russian belief in cruelty and repression as part of a world order ordained by God? And would I have to return to this impenetrable jungle of superstition if I wanted to find my father's roots, and perhaps even my own? Was this the real source of my biography? Was Stalin simply an arbitrary symbol thrown up by this darkness? And was I not much more closely involved in all this than I thought? Were any of the things I thought still true, or was drowning in this darkness an inevitable consequence of trying to penetrate it?

It turned out that my uncle had two sons. One, so he told me, worked at a government office and would look in later on. The other didn't work. With an embarrassed smile, he added that his second son was a drinker. So I had two cousins: Sasha, evidently a civil servant whom I was to meet later on, and Kolya, who apparently belonged to the country's drinking masses and whom I was not to meet later on. Presumably he was just as unwanted in this extremely neat household as I had once been at my father's.

My uncle rummaged about in a drawer and produced a number of faded envelopes, upon which I recognised my father's Russian handwriting. The most recent letter had a date on it that went back five years. A few years after his arrival in Germany, my father had found out where my uncle lived via the company where he worked as a foreman in the engineering department. The letters contained trivial details of life in Germany and were obviously written with the censor in mind. Nonetheless, their tone seemed to reveal a need my father felt to justify his behaviour in fleeing the country. Scanning the meaningless lines of writing, my eyes came to an abrupt halt at the following words: "a young girl I met in Kiev who was innocent in the true sense of the word and whom I brought with me to Germany." Half a page further on I read: "She drowned this year while bathing in a river." For a moment, I believed what I was reading: it sounded so indisputable, so self-evident when you read it like that on the page in my father's even handwriting. For a moment I felt my father hadn't invented the manner of my mother's death at all – I had! Suddenly, I couldn't remember why I had come here. What was I hoping to find? Where was I in this utterly hopeless mess, this farcical family game in which everyone was hiding from everyone else? I didn't even want to see the photograph my uncle was now holding out to me. Something inside me refused. It was like an inner wall of polystyrene, protecting me against this new onslaught on my senses. Who was this woman standing next to my father? Who were these children? There could be little doubt that this was a photo of a young married couple with children. And there could be equally little doubt that my uncle had only shown it to me because it hadn't even occurred to him that my father might have kept his family secret from me. The scales fell from my eyes! Of course! Now it was as clear as day! How could I possibly have believed all this time that my father who was so much older than my mother, so old that I had always been ashamed of him, had always lied about him at the "houses", telling people he was my grandfather – how on earth could I possibly have believed that this man who was almost fifty when I was born, and who therefore really could have been my grandfather, had been a bachelor for almost half a century before he met my mother? In a land where marriage was such an unquestioned institution, in which marriage at an early age was still normal, as were divorce and remarriage.

I held the photo in my hand. I still couldn't grasp what I saw. It was my father with a different woman, and with two children, a boy and a girl. The boy was about seven or eight, and the girl three or four. My father himself wasn't much older than thirty. He was standing next to a dark-haired young woman with a timid smile about her lips. Why had he kept it so secret that he had been married once already in Russia? Why had he kept it in the dark like some crime? Had he only kept it secret from me, or had my mother also known nothing about it? Why did he conceal the truth from everyone? Was it because everything in his later life could be traced back to that "other business" which my uncle refused to divulge out of respect for my father?

I'm holding a photo in my hand. It is at least fifty years old. The little girl on it, my half-sister, may now be one of those prematurely aged little old Russian ladies, and the boy could be almost sixty. On the photo he looks a high-spirited little lad. He's probably been forced by the studio photographer to pose with that basket of flowers in his hand. He's wearing coarse, knitted socks, a Cossack-style shirt tied at the waist, and a neckerchief of the type worn by scouts and Young Pioneers. Between the woman and my father a fat, chubby-cheeked little girl with large, soft dark eyes sits on a kind of column or pedestal, rather like an old-fashioned flower stand. She's wearing knitted socks, too, and a ribbon tied in a big bright bow around her dark, velvet dress. Next to her there's my father on a three-legged stool, his arm thrown about the pedestal on which the little girl is sitting. With a concertina on his knee he'd make the perfect picture of a Russian peasant.

He's wearing an old-fashioned suit that is slightly too big for him, and highly-polished ankle boots. He's sitting with his legs very elegantly crossed, probably at the suggestion of the photographer. He has a peculiar brimmed hat on, similar to the kind worn in traditional Bavarian costume. This rather comical headgear is evidently supposed to be elegant, or snazzy. He has a slight smile on his face. It's a cold smile, but also quite dashing. I notice he's sitting upright with his back as straight as a ramrod, while his free hand is twisted into a deformed, cup-like shape, so that it is difficult to know whether he is merely posing for the photographer, or whether he is demonstrating some sort of special posture, like a soldier at attention. Beside him there's a very gentle, reserved-looking young woman who somehow reminds me of my mother, perhaps because of her full black hair which, like my mother's, is pinned up without the slightest display of vanity. Perhaps it is just her shabby Sunday dress. Or perhaps it is the faint suggestion of terror in her bearing.

My uncle stands behind me and points to the little girl: "Sarah", he says. Then he points to the boy: "David". I start. "And what was their mother's name?" I ask. "I think she was called Bella Daniilovna," replied my uncle. Another typically Russian Jewish name. My thoughts run wild. I watch it slowly dawn on my uncle. "You mean you didn't know that either?" he asks. "So they were Jews?" I ask in return. Obviously feeling uncomfortable now, he shrugs his shoulders: "I think so. I'm not entirely sure." He doesn't answer my other questions. He claims to know nothing about the family, nor whether any of them are still alive. He's only told me their names by mistake, after showing me their photo by mistake, and now he has evidently decided to leave me to the mercy of my own imagination. Right in the middle of the war, with the German Jew-murderers raging throughout the country, my father leaves his Jewish wife and half-Jewish children and goes over to the Nazis with "a young girl" who is "innocent in the true sense of the word". In so doing, he abandons his family not only to the Jew-murderers but also to the reprisals that took place under Stalin's regime of terror, when whole families suffered as a result of one person's "crimes". Did my mother know all this? Was this the reason she had chosen silence, finally opting for silence in its ultimate form? Had she known anything about "that story", which was obviously a different story from the one to which this photograph bore witness, although possibly connected with it in a manner which I couldn't divine. Anything was possible. Perhaps that "other business", that "story", was one of the stories that had occurred thousands, even millions of times under Stalin, when a whole people were suspected of subversion and counter-revolutionary activity. It may have been the story of a victim, a persecutor, an opportunist, or simply the story of a criminal. Perhaps my father really did send his family to their doom, but it could just as easily be true that they were separated long before the war, long before he left the country. It may be a very simple story, of course, the simplest story of all, the story of one of millions of divorces that happen all the time. But if it were really such a simple story, why would my father go to such lengths to keep it secret? Was it just because he had always kept everything secret from me, because everything between us had always remained unspoken? Was that it? Whatever it was, somewhere in his past, which I had begun to unravel in spite of his attempts to conceal it, must lie the source of my father's relentless hatred towards my mother and myself, his second family, whom he had perhaps seen as the embodiment of his dreadful guilt, as the incarnation of the terrible disaster that had befallen him. Or perhaps we simply personified the failure of what was left of his life in a foreign country in which he was hated. He had felt this hatred himself. He had been through two wars, a revolution, a civil war, terror and famine. He had lived through the gigantic inferno that, under the direction of Hitler and Stalin, had left millions in its wake, and my father was perhaps just a worn-out, broken human being whose sole remaining emotion was hatred of all things living. Perhaps he had made my mother and me suffer as a kind of revenge. Perhaps he had avenged his own childhood on me, a childhood of destitution, hunger and violence, a childhood in which he, too, had been homeless. When he looked at me he perhaps saw a girl who was "innocent in the true sense of the word". And unable to bear the sight of an innocence which constantly reminded him of the wrong he had done my mother, he had simply turned the tables, reducing me to the status of a whore. Perhaps this was also his way of exculpating himself for his lust for this young girl who was "innocent in the true sense of the word" – his own daughter. I was all he had, his final possession, and since he possessed nothing else in the world, perhaps he wanted to be absolutely sure of subjugating me. There were no answers to these questions, especially not at my uncle's, the very place it might have been possible to find them. For my uncle was an old man who had probably been sorely tried by his country's frightful history, and who wanted nothing more in life than peace and quiet. Perhaps the portrait of Stalin hanging on his wall showed that he had been unable to keep abreast of his country's history for some time. Perhaps he had once been all too enthusiastic about keeping abreast of it and was now too old and tired to keep up with its furious gallop. Perhaps he had simply become too tired to take the portrait down from the wall. But at least I had found out that I was a cousin, a niece and a half-sister. I had found out that the mother of my half-brother and half-sister was Jewish, and that I wasn't my father's first and only child, but his third. I had found out that my father even kept the truth from his own brother. I had only found out these things through stealth, and because chance had been on my side. But I had also found out that there was more to it than this, that there were some things I was not allowed to know, the most important things. But even finding that out had thrown a faint beam of light upon the darkness of my father's life, upon the grave of his past and therefore also on his present. And it was as though the beam of light had fallen on me too. I had become privy to a secret. It was the secret of a wound. He hadn't hidden the address well enough.

My cousin Sasha has arrived. He's about my age, and looks a bit like my young father on the photo, except that there is nothing peasant-like about Sasha. He's wearing a fashionable, and very elegant summer suit, the kind one never sees on sale in Moscow, and a flashy tie with a raspberry-pink and green pattern on it. On the visiting card he gives me by way of an introduction, I read his first name and family name, my maiden name, in Roman and Cyrillic print, and then the title of his position at the ministry. He is a working-class boy who has evidently worked his way up to a high position in the civil service. He must have spent years training as a cadre and being grounded in ideology. He will obviously have to avoid anything that might be interpreted as a deviation from the party line. It may even be risky for him to meet me here. He tells me the visiting card is only for my own information, and that I should not use the phone number on it to ring him at his office. Without more ado, he opens the bottle of Crimean sparkling wine I bought at the foreign currency shop. We clink glasses, drink. I immediately notice something conspiratorial in his look. His hand accidentally brushes against mine while lighting my cigarette, and something quite inexplicable happens to me. What I find so repulsive about him, and that is nearly everything, exercises an irresistible attraction upon me. I want him to possess me. I want to throw myself at his feet and be totally submissive. I want to be his personal chattel. I no longer belong to myself. I've felt hypnotised ever since he walked through the door. I've become his property. I wait for a signal, one word from him, and I'll submit to him here and now. I'll do anything he wants. At the same time, I hate him. Not because his manner is so avuncular and patronising, as though it were a prodigal daughter he were talking to, a lost sheep who has strayed from the family fold and gone over to the class enemy. I hate him because I am so utterly defenceless against him. It's like an illness, like a delirium. Images of my submission to him alternate in frenzied succession with images of boundless hatred. While this is going on, a line from Else Lasker-Schüler's poem "Eternal Nights" hammers out its pointless rhythm in my mind: "You I've sought incessantly along life's path, but no fellow being has ever shown his face." And beyond that, all I feel is myself going into free fall and the yawning abyss. And because I feel this, because I'm already falling, I want him, this "fellow being", this relative of mine who has made the chasm yawn, who has shown me my own true abyss. I want him to lean out to me across the gulf into which my father has let me fall. I want his violence to hold me fast. I want to melt into it. I want to be able to let myself go, to fall into a hopeless tangle of knots.

Have I not found something here? Have I not found a part of myself? Have I rediscovered my father's daughter? Or the daughter I should have been – his slave, his servant girl, his bondswoman, an object who was supposed to submit to his will? Has that beam of light really penetrated my own darkness? Has it entered my own wound, my deepest, most hidden wound? Haven't my relatives shown me that I am one of them, living in darkness, living in the aura of my father's portrait just like my uncle living under his portrait of "Daddy" Stalin? Haven't they shown me that the freedom of the West has always been much too cold for me? That the thing I had always thought of as the threshold to German life was in fact the place where this freedom begins, a threshold I have never been able to cross because part of me wants to live in bondage, craving the caring safety of captivity? Natalia Gorbanevskaya writes: "In this house of terror where I lie fettered to invisible, eternal chains, I shall feel comfort. And there shall be consolation in the smoke-stained retreat where I lie drunk, poor and bereft of light. For this is where my people live, without guilt, and without the Lord their God."

Yes, I am without guilt. I've done nothing yet to break the law. And I am drunk, too. I am poor and bereft of light in a retreat where I don't have to face my own truth. I am no different from my father. I, too, find consolation in fetters: the fetters of fear. It is the fear of discovering I am alone, of discovering that nobody has power over me, that there is nobody and nothing between myself and God and the universe – no state, no father, no husband.

This is as far as I shall ever get at my uncle's. I realise this as soon as I get down into the dark, empty street where the concrete giants that tower above me look like ocean liners, floating with their lights ablaze through the dark sea of the night. There is nobody about, only a tiny figure shuffling towards me in the distance, recognisable even in the darkness as one of Moscow's little old women. I won't come back here. I'm nothing but an intruder here. Nothing but a stranger. I long to be with Nadya who will be waiting for me in her tiny, two-room flat with its portraits of Pushkin and Heinrich Heine on the walls. I think of my friends in Germany. I think of Günter. I'm taking leave, even if I don't know what from. All I feel is a deep, liberating pain, a pain that has only just begun… The little old woman and I are about to pass each other in the dark, and I want to ask her how to get to the nearest underground station. Just as I'm about to open my mouth, I recognise my aunt. She looks straight past me, her eyes hidden by her headscarf. Her headscarf helps her not to have to see me. She can go home now because I have left.

I don't know whether you're still listening, or even whether this story interests you, a story I must return to as if to a dark dungeon, as if to a time before my pain began. I don't know whether you're listening, and I also don't know who I'm speaking to. Am I addressing a male or a female person? Someone dead or someone alive? Perhaps I'm talking to myself. Perhaps I'm a creature that hasn't been born, that has never seen the light of day. Perhaps I am an embryo in the world's dark belly and have never crawled out to the light. Perhaps I am you, an unfinished being, incapable of living on your own, listening to the waters of the womb through the veil of your prehistoric sleep. How could I have given birth to you when I still hadn't even been born myself? I can only give birth to you through my words, even if these words only express my own unborn state. You are me, and I am you, or I am Captain Nemo, twenty thousand leagues under the sea, surrounded in my "Nautilus" by giant squids and sperm whales. I am what Jules Verne meant when he wrote: "Will the waters one day wash his manuscript ashore and divulge his secret? I do not know. For his sake, all I can do is hope."

I had forgotten all about you, forgotten about you for a long time, for ever. You were nothing but a little red mutilated thing like a frog, floating through an underground network of sewers in a foaming torrent of excrement. And the only image that really made my flesh creep was that of your arrival at the sewage works. It was the thought of you being seen by another person, someone who would know all about you and me, even if he didn't know who I was or where I was. I had a strange image of this witness in my mind. Inevitably, he was a man, a sewage plant worker. He was a rather inconspicuous middle-aged man with receding grey hair. He wore a blue' overall, below which the creases of his grey trousers stood out all the sharper. He had worked in this sewage plant for many years, arriving every day with his briefcase. During his lunch break he took meticulously packed sandwiches out of his briefcase along with a thermos flask of coffee, thin, tasteless coffee like that drunk in families that are always saving money. I didn't know what he actually did at the sewage plant, what his job was, for everything functioned on its own in this subterranean world of sewage. A gigantic and infallible organism automatically divided the good from the bad, the useful from the useless, the pure from the filth. This was a town under the town, in which a supervisor was more or less superfluous, required only for some unforeseeable emergency that had never occurred. What frightened me about him was his inconspicuousness, the faceless grey of his features, the same grey as the sewage itself. What frightened me was his face, which was indistinguishable from other faces, identical to all the other faces I saw in the town. In each of these faces I recognised my witness, my accessory. Each of them had seen you floating past, a red frog-like thing in an infernal river of faeces and sludge, hardly distinguishable from the rest of the excrement and yet immediately picked out by his expert eyes which were trained to spot anything unusual. I had been running away from him from the moment I saw you enter the sewers. I saw him coming round every corner, emerging from every house, the president of the subterranean sewage plant, the king of emergencies, one of which had at last happened. I wanted to meet him head on. I wanted to give myself up in the hope of being delivered of my terrible secret. And eventually he recognised me and seized me, dashing me to pieces with the steel hook of his hand. Or he wept. At last, someone to weep with, over you, the mutilated, drowned child that I was, for whom no one had ever grieved, the dead child that I am, the child I hope to find in the Acheron of this story.

The Easter holidays were over and I was back at school. I felt grateful to my father. In fact I felt something like devotion towards him. After all, he hadn't killed me; he had let me live. He had unlocked the door of my room. Perhaps it had even been open for some time without my knowing. In any case, I had found it open and somehow managed to get to the tap. At first I couldn't even drink. It took me some time to learn how to swallow again, how to move my jaws, how to use my gums and tongue, the muscles in my mouth. I only gradually learned how to breathe again, how to move my fingers and toes. I couldn't feel any teeth in my mouth when I tried to chew bread. I couldn't find the hole for the bulky bits of food to get down, for the water which, at first, felt neither wet nor liquid; for the air which, at first, felt full of needles. After a while I began to regain the use of my joints, sinews and muscles, and I saw a face in the mirror which, with some effort, I recognised as my own. And I began to get used to the idea that I was going to survive and that nothing had changed.

The evening before I went back to school, I waited for my father to go off on his late shift, then forged his signature on my report. While I was looking for an example of his signature in the kitchen table drawer where he kept his papers, I noticed that the money he always kept there was gone. I remembered the five marks I had stolen. Obviously, this had made my father decide to hide his savings and weekly wages from me. I also remembered the money I had stolen as a child. I had started with ten *pfennigs* from my mother's purse, which she kept in the same drawer, to buy an "American" ice cake from the baker's on my way to school in the morning. Then, as my courage grew, I took twenty *pfennigs*, then thirty, so that I could buy marshmallows, waffles and coloured pens that I needed for school and was never given any money for. Eventually I started taking fifty *pfennigs*, for which you could get a lovely piece of Dutch cherry tart. For a few weeks like this I led a secret, double life, wallowing in sweet abundance, surprised how easy it was, how painlessly one could come by riches. But one day when I came home from school, my mother was standing in front of the kitchen table with the face I feared most, a face which seemed to consist solely of fiery cheeks and mad eyes that shot vicious bolts of lightning at me. I was told to go down to the cellar and fetch the axe. I knew why, of course. It was because liars had their tongues cut out and thieves had their hands chopped off. I went for the axe as to the scaffold, indeed as though I were already dead. And years later I was still plagued by the horrific image of my two hands lying hacked off in the drawer. They lay next to each other at the scene of my crime, cold and stiff, as though the drawer were their grave.

His own name was the only word my father could write in German. I found his signature written in a beginner's hand under his photograph in his stateless person's passport. Copying these simple letters, which he himself had had to copy, was child's play, and the only thing I had to practise was the sweeping flourish that suddenly shot out from the final, stiffly composed letter of his signature. But I soon mastered his hand, got inside that spontaneous hand-flick which was always directed at me as if it were the logical extension of whatever my father happened to be doing at the time.

I had always managed to lie to my father. I had one decided

advantage over him: the German language. I knew he couldn't
go to my school and ask about my report. Although he had
lived in Germany for almost twenty years, he could hardly
speak a word of German. Since my mother's death I had acted
as an interpreter for him. I had filled in forms whose questions
seemed to come from a different planet. I had accompanied
him as an interpreter to the offices of various municipal
authorities. Even as a ten-year-old, I had had to answer official
correspondence in my squiggly child's handwriting, my father
dictating the replies to me in Russian, expecting me to
translate his words as I wrote. Although these were my father's
replies, they were not replies to the letters themselves, but to
what I had translated into Russian for him from German
officialese, while I endeavoured to translate my father's
Russian replies into the appropriate German. These corres-
pondences frequently dragged on for weeks and months,
becoming so confused in the process that the German
authorities were eventually forced to give up. Once, we got a
letter from the building society that owned the "houses" and I
thought it said that we were going to be paid a large sum of
money. My father then dictated a reply to me, inquiring when
and where he could collect the money. A large number of
letters were then exchanged, their contents reaching such a
degree of confusion that one day a furious gentleman from
the building society paid us a personal visit, demanding my
father pay cash for a supplementary rent bill we had
apparently neglected for months. But usually my father's
shameful ignorance of the language was to my advantage. He
could hit me, lock me up or torture me in his attempt to
squeeze a confession out of me. He could even kill me if he
wanted to. But he couldn't go to my German school and ask
whether I'd been given a report; or rather, he couldn't prove
that I had been given one, even though it was practically

self-evident. He couldn't go to anyone at the "houses" for proof that I had been lying since I was the only one there who went to a grammar-school. If it had come to it, I would simply have maintained that grammar-school reports were handed out at different times from reports at normal schools. Our whole German environment was an insoluble riddle to my father. Its customs, manners and habits were a closed book to him. I could tell him whatever I wanted and get away with it. I could pull the wool over his eyes whenever I chose. And even if he didn't believe me, even if he was quite sure I was lying, once I had survived his beatings and torments he was quite powerless against the reality I invented. Language was my advantage. Even in those days language was my refuge, the only place I could stand my ground. It was my sole form of defence, the only weapon I had.

I had nothing to fear at school for having forged my father's signature. Nobody there knew my father's signature, and nobody was ever going to see it. The gulf between the Germans and ourselves was my salvation in situations like this. In this gulf, which was also a gulf between the two centres of authority over me, I had acquired a certain freedom of movement. I felt quite at home in this no-man's-land between hostile powers. This was my hiding place.

Mr Schwarz, our history teacher and a ruthless interrogator of facts, dates and names, especially with poorer pupils like myself, strode up and down in front of the blackboard in his black, horn-rimmed spectacles, his mouth emitting a kind of loud, barking noise, waving his cane in the air to underline the significance of each syllable of his delivery. I could expect his cane to pick me out at any moment. Like an arrow homing in on a bull's eye it was bound to catch me out and prove me guilty of ignorance. In fact there was no point in my sitting here at all. There wasn't the slightest hope that I would pass the lower-school final exams and get my school-leaving certificate. My brain felt full of cement. I could feel a sort of dead weight rising behind my eyes, like pastry, or like a mountain of lead. I had never experienced school as anything but a machine designed to grind me down and crush my will. The material we were taught was like some foreign body implanted in my own body by means of a never-ending series of operations. It was like being force-fed something to make you vomit. Of all the stuff I had drummed into my head – and I did so for the sole purpose of getting pass-marks and a presentable report – nothing had stuck in my mind at all. On the contrary, the longer I went to school the stranger the world became. School didn't break down the wall between me and the world about me. It just made it thicker, denser. School turned life into dead matter, turned the world into an unbelievably bleak and barren planet, a desert, an object from which I had become totally estranged and which had never seemed to have any bearing on me whatsoever. School was a machine which multiplied all my feelings of being different, of being excluded and Russian. From my very first day there I had been pilloried, exposed to public view, pelted with scorn. They had poured derision on everything: on my haircut, my ears, my calf-muscles, my way of walking, my way of standing and my clothes. This laughter was worse than – and had also outlived – all the other forms of humiliation I had suffered as a child, when they had kicked me and punched me and driven me through the playground. As a child I had lived in permanent fear of being chased, of the totally unrelated incidents that would suddenly, with neither rhyme nor reason, spark off their explosive aggression after school. It would come straight out of the blue, without the slightest provocation on my part. They would suddenly come racing after me like hounds after a fox, baying and yelling their war-cries: "Russki, Russki". They were a little mob of avenging angels and butchers, a gang of little racists and revanchists. I was an outlaw, whereas they were above the law. They had right on their side. In fact, they were simply *right*! They were the incarnation of justice, chasing me through the streets, screaming, spouting venom, spitting, throwing dirt and stones after me. I would run for my life. Desperately gasping for breath, I would make for the "houses", for the dried-out bed of the canal which marked the border between Germany and the East. Here, they left off chasing me at last, since they knew this was where their own territory ended and the leper colony began. The only thing that had survived from these hunts was their derisive laughter, but the laughter was the worst of all. It seemed to have doubled in potency since our return from the school holidays. The reason for this lay somewhere between the beginning of the holidays and my imprisonment by my father. I especially noticed it in Manuela's eyes, in the knowing looks she gave me which betrayed that she knew something about me that I didn't know myself, something which perhaps lay at the bottom of the dark abyss into which the train in which I was travelling had plunged that evening at the "Moonlight" pub. It was a gap in my memory in which a part of me was lost. Since then I had felt as though there were a hole in my skin, and it wasn't only Manuela but a whole class of scornful, mocking faces who seemed able to look through it at something dreadful, which I had every reason to feel ashamed of, but which only I couldn't see. Since that evening, or even before then, ever since my evening at the German "Linden", ever since my first fleeting contact with the distant world I had longed so much to be part of, the world in which I had first met Achim Uhland, my feelings of insecurity had increased drastically. Something in me had become visible, something had finally exposed me to ridicule, to a shame that far exceeded any I had felt before. My love for a German boy was considered ridiculous. Yes, that was it! It was simply considered ridiculous! And I squirmed with shame over my insuperable desire to be loved back. My desire to be loved by Achim Uhland had remained insuperable even after he'd called me a "Russian slut". In fact, since then it had become even worse. It had turned into an obsession. I had fallen head over heels – only to meet with his contempt. It was like falling into a pool of petrol which was constantly burning with my desperation. And the only hope I saw was to win his love in spite of everything. For not to be loved by him was to be finally sentenced to death by the German world.

Mr Schwarz's cane had picked me out just as I thought it would – like an arrow hitting the bull. I stood in front of the class and was supposed to fill the gaping void of the blackboard with white letters. But I hadn't even understood the question I was meant to be answering! At a complete loss, I looked around to see if anyone in the class could help me. I saw myself through the others' eyes. I was nothing but skin and bone with hollow eyes, swaying like a branch in the wind when I had to stand up for any length of time. It was as if the sinews had been drawn from my body, as if I lacked an inner axis to hold me together. Having searched in vain for help among the rows of my fellow-pupils, my eyes fixed upon the square of a high window where there really was a bare, dead branch swaying in the grey rain, and from that moment I knew my schooldays were over. And since my schooldays were over, my life at the "houses" was over too. Everything was over: school, which forced me to return to my father at the "houses", and my father at the "houses" who forced me to go to school. Whatever happened to me out there where the branch swayed in the grey rain, it couldn't be much worse than what I'd had to put up with already. Out there! Out there was where life began! Here, I was already dead. I had never lived here. Something would turn up out there. Achim Uhland was out there somewhere. At least there was a possibility out there, whereas in here there was nothing but certainty, the certainty of my downfall.

I still wasn't here when countries
were still fatherlands . . .
I was still dead when the big wars began . . .

hereafter a roaring will kill us
raging through the world in white stillness
recognised by no one –

Wolfgang Hilbig

Out there! But what was "out there" in those days? A time
dropped from the calendar. The rubble and ruins of the
aftermath long gone, and the era of students' revolt still far
away. An interim period, an interval between the acts, an hour
fallen from the face of a clock, a carriage shunted onto a
siding. The prolongation of a period Heinrich Böll called the
second destruction of Germany, following the war: the
reconstruction, the *Wirtschaftswunder*. The dawn, the
twilight of the gods of a consumer dictatorship. The heyday of
the "upright citizen". The unbroken triumph of a smothering
silence that lay like a blanket over everything. The memory of
being buried alive. Apparently, the whole of Germany was a
province in those days. But then what were the provinces
themselves in Germany? And what was a refugee ghetto in one
of those provinces? A province in the provinces of a province?
Everything felt enclosed, hemmed in, immured in silence.

Yes, in those days we were all prisoners, walled in behind a nation's silence. Causing rows, yelling, getting drunk and smashing the place up didn't help, either. When the noise died down the hush was as deathly as ever. Although it was loud, too. Everyone was rushing about madly, frantically grabbing whatever they could get. Everything was being improved and embellished and refined. The Federal Republic of Germany was one big beauty parlour! And how lucky we were to have a chemist's on the High Street of our provincial town where for a few pence you could have yourself immersed in a cloud of eau de Cologne, sprayed on by some gushing, overzealous chemist! New smells from perfume bottles, tubes of wax polish, packets of scouring powder and Persil had covered over all kinds of things I didn't even know about. All I knew was what it felt like to be covered over. I was what had to be sprayed over, spruced up, washed out and scoured away. And if they really did hate everything that reminded them of their past, then they obviously had good reason to hate refugees from the East more than anything else, and the Russians in particular. This hatred spread to their children, who had no idea why they hated us; it was simply part of the air they breathed. We children were enemies without knowing why. We were actors in a shadow panto-mime whose plot we didn't know.

How quickly they had forgotten. Not only those they had murdered, but also their own dead, their own hunger, their own ruins, their own fear, even their own skins, which they'd only just saved. It was as if they had found new, substitute skins in Nyltest and Trevira synthetics. And there was nothing in the world I wanted more than to be like them, to be loved for the Nyltest and Trevira skin which I couldn't buy. I so wanted to be like them that becoming German seemed to me to be the only means of becoming fully human, and it is the story of this confusion I am really telling here. I am getting close to the darkest part of this story. I feel afraid. I take refuge in books about the period. I'm on the run. I read everything I can. I find out everything there is to know about myself – and find nothing. I'm going to have to tell it myself. Nobody will tell it for me. But first I must find it. I must find the right words, for in finding the words one finds the things they refer to. And one never knows whether one fails because of the words or because of the things themselves. The space between words and things, expressed in terms of the space between the writer and a sheet of paper, is like a cleft in the earth which can swallow up the writer at any moment. It is the presence of this fatal cleft that writers must endure in everything they do.

Let me read about the period. I'll allow myself just one more day's reading. Then another. Just one more tiny procrastination. I read: "First revaluation of the Deutschmark", and "Adenauer re-elected Chancellor". "National service extended", I read, and "Eichmann executed". I read about the beginning of the "*Spiegel* Affair". "Hermann Hesse dead", I read. "Nabokov's *Lolita* and Bergmann's *Silence* new box-office hits", I read, and "Campaign to Clean up the Screen". "It is almost impossible to imagine quite how conservative the literature of family counselling and sex education was in those days," I read, and "a number of art scandals revealed the potentially explosive aggressive urges behind the mental repression, taboos, prudery and exaggerated moral standards of the fifties." In Michael Schneider's essay "A Post-War Childhood" I read: "The accidents and anonymous, hostile forces that seemed to be waiting for me around every corner were figments not only of my own, but also of the collective imagination. They were the fantasies of an historical epoch in which a whole nation felt itself threatened by the world enemy number one. For us children, that enemy was 'the Russians'!" I read novels, reports and stories, diaries kept during the period by women and girls. I flick through magazines and beauty guides, and watch TV films full of lisping, hip-wiggling, eyelash-fluttering *fräuleins* of the economic miracle years, out to catch their husband in Tirol or wherever. And perhaps by recreating the Germany of that era I can also make the person I was then more real to myself. Because when I speak of her, I'm really talking about someone I don't know, a missing person, a mere phantom of my memory. I'm talking about someone I've lost touch with, although I've no idea when I lost touch with her. Or perhaps it was she who lost touch with me. Either she rejected me, or I rejected her. We got separated somehow, and now neither of us knows where the other is. And I don't know which of us is suffering. Is she suffering because she's lost me? Or am I suffering because I've lost her?

Above all else, "out there" was an arena for the "potentially explosive aggressive urges" of those days, and the girl I want to talk about in the darkest part of this story was their perfect target. She really did end up running away from school and home. She had nowhere to stay, a sixteen-year-old homeless person in a provincial boom-town. She was seen all over the place by an awful lot of people, the way it is when one sleeps around the town on park benches and attic floors, and when the only hope of survival is the hope of getting married. That, at least, was one thing she had in common with the German provincial *fräuleins* of the fifties. But I'm so far away from her that I can hardly remember any of it. Perhaps that's not true. Perhaps I'm just too close to see her. I see the river, and the river itself is much clearer to me than the image of myself beside the river. It is as if I were looking at *my* Volga, as if the air there smelled of my father's childhood and youth, and as if this smell had merged with the smell of my own childhood.

My memory of the river is a memory of something that existed before I was there. The river is a part of me, just as my mother has become a part of the river. The river flows through the strange melancholy of the Russian folk songs that we sang in the kitchen in the evenings – my mother, my father and I, sitting at the open windows, in which the warm twilight was like a web of golden threads whose lustre was slowly dying, slowly drowning in the mist that rose from the river. If I have any memory of happiness at all, it is this memory of singing with my parents, when my father and mother were miraculously united, and when I was miraculously united with them. And perhaps it was only while singing that I didn't feel alone. Blissfully unaware of myself, I would surrender to the three-part harmony, my voice taking its place between the deep, bell-like accompaniment of my father, from which everything cold and menacing had disappeared, and my mother's soprano, which, no longer dragged down by her sense of doom, imitated the voice of a Russian peasant girl and described a series of high arcs above my own alto part:

> Over the river yonder
> A red glow ends the day.
> O dearest weeping willow
> Take my pain away.
> O little willow weeping,
> Your green head mutely bowed,
> He is gone for ever
> Whom I to love have vowed.

We scooped buckets of water from the river for the allotment that fed us in summer. And the current seemed to carry me along as I ran with the cool, damp grass of the riverbank under my bare feet. Far away I ran, no matter where, my eye following the course of the river to where a vast green gate opened in the sky above the distant, misty horizon. Along the riverbanks were the small drooping weeping willows whose green, shaggy tresses hung down and were rinsed, combed and tousled again by the current. We stood by the river one Christmas Eve with the frost crunching under our feet, lured out onto the bridge by the furious wailing of police sirens. We stood there mute and muffled, titillated by the horror of it all, gazing down into the black water where two lights had appeared, and where a crane was hoisting up the wreck of a crashed car whose headlamps were still shining, but whose driver sat dead at the wheel. In summer, whenever I roamed through the bushes at the edge of the river, I always expected to meet a particularly eerie image from one of Pushkin's poems:

> Home from the beach the children ran,
> Calling their father, pulling his hand.
> Quick, father! Quick! As fast as you can!
> For in our nets we've caught a dead man.

And the power of the river – in another poem by Pushkin the river is called the Neva and floods the huts of the poor who live on its banks in St. Petersburg – this great power threatened to overwhelm us, too, one rainy summer. It rose over its banks and flooded our vegetable patches; then started to creep towards our front door. Soaked and exhausted, we waded about for a while in the quagmire among the tomatoes and potatoes. Eventually, we were forced to accept that there was nothing we could do to rescue that year's harvest. We would simply have to eat even less than usual. The streams and puddles on the low ground had joined to form a single, smooth patch of water behind the blocks where we lived.

Though it stretched as far as the eye could see, this patch of water looked quite harmless at first, like a lake. But the rain didn't let up. It fell for weeks on end, until the lake began to bubble and seethe. Powerful little currents formed, whirlpools, rapids, uncanny reminders of the river itself, which was coming closer and closer, and which had swollen to a mighty, roaring torrent that tore out trees and dragged along bushes and stones, a raging, dirty brown mass, sweeping away everything in its path. It came perilously close, and was already licking at the foundations of the first flats. There was nothing we could do, so we leant anxiously out of our windows and talked incessantly about the river. But in our mind's eye each of us was already snatching this and that from our drawers and cupboards, hurriedly packing little bundles of belongings to take with us on our flight. Months later, long after the river had retreated to its normal course, leaving our gardens devastated in its wake, the rain would wake me at night. The first drops of rain that hit my window were like a signal. I would immediately wake up and hear, against the rustle of the rain outside, the sound of water rising, the sound of the river seething, swelling, coming closer. Petrified, I watched it trickle through the cracks in my walls. And then it burst into my room, engulfing me, dragging me along in its raging torrent. How could I have known that one day the river really would swallow our house! But then of course I knew! I had always known that my mother was gradually withdrawing, leaving me for the river. The river had caught her eye, and soon she had eyes only for the river. She no longer saw me. The river was taking her away from me, bit by bit. Finally, when there was hardly any of her left, the river took the last little snippet.

After the flood, nobody really felt like recultivating the

gardens on the flatlands down by the river. Either that, or they no longer had any time for hobbies. For the German economic miracle had attracted half of Europe's poor. It had depopulated whole villages in Andalusia and Calabria. Suddenly, Germany couldn't get enough even of *us*, although we had previously known little more than its cold shoulder. And so anyone who could grabbed a job doing piece-work at a conveyor-belt, hoping the wages would be enough to buy them a little bit of life while the going was good, a little bit of Germany, which you could only get for hard cash.

My father had also given up his garden after my mother's death, and soon there were only a few, half over-grown gardens left scattered on the deserted riverside behind the "houses". There was also a rotting, semi-derelict shed where I had often spent the night since running away from home and school.

Every morning when I get to the end of the gravel track and step out onto the High Street, my metamorphosis begins. I have to adapt my inner self to my outward appearance. Or to be more exact, I have to transform myself inwardly in order to believe in my outward appearance. I imagine myself as Manuela, or as the daughter of a German doctor, or as a famous film star, the kind of person everyone in a small German town reveres. As intensely as I can, I imagine a particular German girl I know, and I keep on imagining her until I feel her gestures become my own, until I feel myself walking and smiling like her, until I feel I'm wearing the same dress and hairstyle as her. And only at the very back of my mind do I know how I really look. My frilly American dress still hasn't dried after being washed in the river. Far too short for me and far too wide, the yellow Perlon hangs off me all tattered and torn, covered in stubborn tar and rust stains. I wear my shiny red belt as tightly as possible, gathering the loose material into what is supposed to look like a fashionable wasp waist. The worn-out American high heels into which I have forced my chilblained feet make me wince with pain at every step, turning my gait into a strangely pretentious skip or limp, but also leaving me with no choice but to sway my hips in the prescribed manner, at once sexy and restrained. The cheap creamy pink I wear on my lips, a lipstick I found on the street, is a smear on a face whose hollow eyes and cheeks spell out my hunger for all to see. Attempting to imitate Manuela, I've back-combed my hair as high as it will go; but instead, it's become a weird sort of pyramid and looks like dirty, ruffled plumage. Short bouts of raucous coughing shake me at regular intervals, making my breastbone feel rough and splintered. I've had nothing to eat but a few raw vegetable leaves and small green potatoes, eaten ravenously along with their earth and leaves and stolen at dawn from one of the few remaining cultivated patches down by the river. Thus I step out onto the High Street of this small German town, whatever doubts I have dispelled as quickly as they arrive by the overriding necessity of appearing attractive to German crafts-men, of being beautiful and worthy of marriage. Waiting all day for the evening to come is a torture. Driven by hunger, I wander about the streets and alleys until the shops close and the High Street at last fills with life again, becoming a promenade for the boys and girls of the town and surrounding villages. I gaze enviously at the few boys and girls who have already found partners and who arrive on the scene as couples. I hear people say: "They're going steady!" And it's true! Hand in hand, slowly, in an almost stately manner, they walk up and down the High Street from the Capitol cinema at one end, to Parade Square at the other. These girls look very different from the rest of us who haven't been chosen yet. The smiles on their faces are subdued, given over entirely to relishing their elect status. Their petticoats don't bob up and down quite so obviously as ours when they walk, and the measured tread of their snow-white stiletto heels on the pavement has a regal dignity which only they possess. In fact, they don't really belong here any more at all. They are beyond having to show themselves on the High Street in the evenings. Their only function here is to provide the rest of us with the sublime perspective of the destination once reached. "This is what it's like," say their eyes, say the little gestures of happiness with which they lean their heads on their partners' shoulders as they pass, "this is what it looks like when you are someone's girlfriend or fianceé and are soon to be a bride, and when you no longer need give a damn about winning anyone's favour because you've already got it." And the secret of these girls, the thing that immediately strikes you, is that they're incredibly sexy and incredibly respectable at the same time. That's my new magic word: sexy! In order to get married you have to be not only respectable and modest, in other words a virgin; you also have to be sexy. They didn't tell us anything about that at convent! On the contrary, if a girl was sexy it meant she was depraved and dirty and that no man would ever want to marry her. But I soon realised that things were quite different in real life. The girls most likely to have found a fiancé were also those who were most capable of performing a highly delicate balancing act between two opposites: respectability and sex appeal. I saw it was a question of dosage. There was a mysterious recipe for the concoction of the ideal blend, the only blend suitable for marriage. A drop too much of this or a drop too little of that could ruin everything. It was evidently their exact knowledge of this correct dosage, of this finest of balances between respectability and sex appeal, that was the source of the utterly enviable, and yet wholly inscrutable confidence which the chosen few radiated from every pore of their bodies, and which, for them, turned promenading on the High Street into nothing less than a victory parade.

I could never be sure which of the two I lacked more – respectability or sex appeal? Sometimes it was one, sometimes the other. Surely it had something to do with my sex appeal that I had been considered so frivolous and dissolute at convent. Surely it had something to do with my sex appeal that my father called me a whore, and Achim Uhland a Russian slut. On the other hand, it seemed to be my very lack of sex appeal, the totally sexless backwardness of my convent upbringing, coupled with my peculiar Russian backwardness, which made me such an uninteresting match. Whenever I strolled past the German craftsmen, I never knew whether it was better to stiffen my hips as I walked and lower my eyes as respectably as I could, so as not to look too sexy, or to smile with all the sex appeal I could muster and to sway my hips as seductively as I could so as not to appear too respectable.

Occasionally, a German craftsman even puts my marriage-ability to the test. First he strolls along beside me for a while or takes me for a ride on his moped. Later, by the park or down by the woods, I have to let him kiss me to prove how grown-up and sexy I am. I'm not quite sure whether I manage to prove this though. I don't know whether I'm supposed to enjoy kissing or whether I may have even failed the first part of the test because I find the German craftsman revolting. I found the wet kisses of adults revolting when I was little, too, but now my revulsion has taken on a monstrous life of its own inside me. Trying not to choke, I swallow a horrible jelly-like substance, a spider's spawn that gushes from the German craftsman's mouth and pours into me while he's hugging me and kissing me – well, not exactly hugging, but doing something that bends me over backwards and crushes me, like my father's arms forcing me to swim in the river and keeping me underwater. Only this time it isn't water but jelly, a torrent of spider's spawn pouring out of the German craftsman and entering my body. And it won't be long before I feel the spawn move inside me. The spider will suddenly start jerking about right in the middle of the High Street with the whole town watching, and want out. The spider's grown inside me without me knowing, grown into a huge, black monster with hairy legs as thick as levers, pumping away inside me, wanting out. And I'll start running, fleeing in panic, chased by a wild, yelling mob. I'll have the whole town after me. I'll run like I did when I was little and they were throwing stones at me. I'll run back to the shelter of the "houses" and my shed by the river. I'll hide myself, entrench myself in my shed, and once I'm really there, invisible, so invisible nobody can get at me, the spider inside me will gradually lie down under the spasmic blows of the burning cough I've got from running, a cough so hot it seems to be melting my breastbone. I'll crawl under the rags and cardboard of my bed on the rotting floor of the shed and wait until morning; until hunger tears me from my sleep and drives me back out onto the High Street. Perhaps everything will repeat itself the following day. I'll get another German craftsman to pick me up and put me to the test. It's a survival test. Once I've proved how grown-up and sexy I am, once I'm choking on his jelly, I'll finally be allowed to prove how respectable I am. Finally I'll be allowed to feel revolted. In fact, I'm supposed to feel revolted. It's the second part of the test. As soon as the German craftsman tries to put his hand down the neck of my dress, or force his hand up under my skirt, I'm allowed to feel at one with the storm of revulsion that rages inside me. The more disgusted I feel, the more respectable I am. Although I'm not exactly sure what I'm supposed to be defending myself against, or what it is the

German craftsman wants of me, because my notions of what he might be after are confined to those I have managed to glean from my fifties' convent upbringing: the wildest, most fantastic visions possible, whose function at the convent was to keep a wall between us and knowledge. For mere contact with knowledge of this kind was the beginning of sin. A person who knew had left innocence behind her. A person who knew was already a part of iniquity. The smell of profanity exuded from such a person, just as it did from those who had already been punished with the stigmas of their sex: periods, and the first bulging of their breasts. And the fact that these changes may have occurred against their will was irrelevant; they were powerless against the sin that was innate in them. The most innocent pupils were the late developers and physically retarded girls who knew nothing or next to nothing, of whom I was one. This single advantage I had over others was a source of pride and consolation to me, but also of constant fear and suspicion of my own body. For my body was a liar. Its harmless, innocent appearance was a veil for the acts of wantonness I committed at night, for the mortal sins which I hid from my Catholic confessor, and which already meant I was condemned to go to hell as a desecrator of Christ's body. But my assurance of being evil also gave me a certain obscure sense of satisfaction. The evil in me made me strong. It made me invincible. It provided me with armour. It was a weapon against the power of good which – because I was excluded from it – threatened to suffocate me. So although I didn't exactly know what I was supposed to be defending myself against in the second part of the test, and although I didn't know whether a German craftsman really could have something quite as dirty as a sexuality that was related in some abstruse manner to my own, a relationship, in other words, to the dirt in me, to my innate sinfulness that was full to the brim with the substance of the spider, what I did know was that I was defending myself against this relationship. And I knew that if I didn't defend myself, this relationship, which really was all that existed between me and the German craftsman, would consummate something which my father had begun. Indeed, perhaps it had been consummated long ago, and perhaps the reason why I didn't know this was because it had been swallowed by the darkness into which my mother's arms once wrenched me. And the more violent the German craftsman became, the more clearly my body began to recognise something essentially paternal in him, something which was therefore a natural part of my environment, like all forms of violence. Force had not only been the natural law governing my existence until now, it had also been the star under which I had been furtively sired on a dirty camp bed under the Nazis. But perhaps there was more to it than simply the violence of the times. Perhaps I had been engendered by force, becoming the incarnation of this violence in my mother's body. And the more violent the German craftsman became, the more I felt he was not trying to break through to what was respectable in me, but merely to what was abject, and that this was not a means of putting me to the test, but merely a means of stamping me as a reject. Perhaps I was not worth putting to the test since I had nothing to prove in the first place. In my case, everything was obvious from the start, obvious to the craftsman I'd been with the day before, obvious to the one I'd been with the day before that, obvious to my father, to Achim Uhland, and even to myself, since I'd never had anything to prove but my depravity and filthiness. And yet I still hoped the German craftsman might have some reason to expect proof to the contrary as he forced me down into the wet grass by the forest, onto stones and branches that stuck into my back, as he threw his heavy, panting body on top of me, giving me a final chance to show him how far I was prepared to go to resist him, a final chance to become his girlfriend, his fianceé, his bride to be, a chance to become everything the word "German" embraced, everything that was the opposite of me and which was therefore impossible for me to prove to the German craftsman. For all I could prove was that I could scratch better, bite better and use my fists better than German girls, although they ate well and were respectable, whereas I was as hungry and as rude as a stray dog.

Sometimes I manage to get into my father's house through a door that someone has forgotten to lock and spend the night in the attic, which is like heaven on earth to me, especially when it's raining. Perhaps I've come straight from stealing in the German gardens, where I sometimes go at night to get a few green apples and pears which I quickly stuff down my front, always ready to make a dash for it as soon as a dog barks or a window lights up, my hands shaking with anticipation as they clutch their treasures under my dress. Or perhaps I've just come from stealing in the German fields on the other side of the river, where I rob the German cows and pigs of their maize and turnips. Or perhaps I've just been up on the High Street waiting in vain for the German craftsman. Or I've just been in my father's flat, for which I've discovered a key, a key I secretly use when he's not in, although he's known about this for ages. And whenever I manage to get into the attic – that is, when the attic door has been left unlocked as well – I wrap myself up for the night in my mother's old clothes from the sack that my father once got rid of up here and has long since forgotten. I've even found a torn mattress under the junk, and some flattened cardboard boxes which I pull over me as blankets. My father doesn't know I'm up here. On the other hand, I can't really be sure he doesn't know. Perhaps he knows everything there is to know and that's why he doesn't come looking for me. In fact, no one seems to be looking for me at all; not my father, nor anyone from school, which I've simply left without trace, nor the German police. It's as if I had never existed and as if everything I've run away from had never existed. Until very recently I'd been forbidden to set foot outside my father's flat. Even walking through the town to school was only tolerated as a necessary evil. I had always been forbidden to go walking on the German streets. Initially, it had been because I was too little, and later, because I wasn't little enough. And suddenly I've become the freest person there is on those streets. I can do whatever I want. Nobody bothers about me. Nobody even seems to have noticed that I'm missing. My absence has disturbed absolutely nothing! It's like when my mother stopped watching over me and I was suddenly free of all ties overnight. And I'm amazed, just as I was then, by the weird state of anarchy this entails; and just as there was then, there seems to be something building up behind my back, like a slow but steady trickle of water that may suddenly burst and engulf me. I don't think of the future, of what's going to happen to me, or of how I'm going to stay alive like this. I'm just letting myself drift. And even though gnawing hunger keeps me awake at night, I'm happy. At last I'm simply drifting. At last I've cut myself loose. I've got away and am drifting towards life as a German adult. Of that I am certain! I lie awake in the attic and my hunger, like my revulsion, has taken on a monstrous life of its own. It's like a plant, like an animal sucking at me, feeding on me. My body has become a battlefield for two warring elements: hunger and revulsion. Sleep consists only of brief moments of respite into which I plunge violently and noisily, starting up again in horror, surrounded by galleries of white washing drying in a moonlit attic. Were those steps I heard? Isn't that the drunken, gasping breath of my father coming up the stairs, the sound of heavy breathing coming closer and closer, step by step, getting louder and louder until I realise it's my own breathing banging away like something trapped inside a bottle. I feel under the cardboard cover that keeps me warm for the key I carry under my dress. It's through this key that my father knows about me. Perhaps he even knows that I lead a secret life under his roof, not only when he's away by day, but also at night; the life of a thief, of a parasite, a life no different from that of the hordes of mice that led invisible lives behind the walls and ceilings of our flat, and whose wild rumblings frightened me as a child when I lay in bed and listened.

One rainy night when the attic was locked and the prospect of spending the night on the cold wet floor of the shed filled me with dread, I crawled into the boiler in the laundry room. I had remembered a story of homeless children that my mother had once told me, orphans who led the lives of vagabonds in the Soviet Union during the Civil War. These children were famous for having slept in tar boilers at night, where the hardened tar was still warm enough to prevent them from freezing to death. And true enough, there was still a little warmth in the enamel on the inside of the laundry boiler! Somebody had obviously done their washing that day! I curled up under the iron lid, clasping my arms and legs so firmly to my body that I became as tiny as a circus acrobat in a magic box. The next morning I woke up frozen solid. I'd become part of the boiler, like a fossil. I couldn't move and I couldn't get out. I was trapped under the black lid. It was on that morning that the key fell into my hands. It quite literally fell into my hands as I reeled and wedged myself against the laundry door like some screwed-up object, and I don't know why, but I immediately knew that the rusty key in my hand was a miracle, a godsend. My father's bicycle was gone from under the stairs in the cellar, so I knew he was out on his late shift. The key turned easily in the lock of my father's flat, and soon I was thawing out under the blankets in my own room. As the warmth entered my body, I began to shiver. It was like a generator starting up inside me, shaking me back to life. Strangely, I didn't even catch a cold that night, nor during any of the nights that followed. Though the summer months were among the rainiest and coldest there had been for many years, my body held out till the end. And even if we're still a long way from the end of this story, I was drifting inexorably towards it that morning in my father's flat, which had opened to me like Sesame to Aladdin's magic lamp. The larder in my father's kitchen had opened to me, too, and it remained open. That was what was so inexplicable! It was my salvation, but it was also uncanny. My father knew what I was up to, and yet he let me have my way. He even seemed to be giving me his support, although my behaviour must have deserved the death penalty in his eyes. He had only to wait for me to come to his flat one day, had only to move his bicycle from its usual place in the cellar to make me think he was out on late or early shift, and he could have seized me without any trouble at all! He had only to change the lock on the door of his flat! Sooner or later hunger would have broken me, and he would have had me back under his thumb. But he left everything wide open. And I couldn't understand why!

Sometimes I felt that my father and I had finally made it up with one another. It was as if he had secretly decided to give me my freedom. Sometimes I felt overcome by strange feelings of affection towards him. It was like love for a stranger who returned my love and gave me his support. His love and support were a sign that I had taken my mother's place at his side. I was his companion, his wife. I had briefly felt something similar after my mother's death. I had thought of myself then as her substitute, her successor. I had thought he would pay more attention to me, acknowledge my existence at last. I had felt it was perhaps only my mother's constant presence that had prevented him from noticing me in the first place. Her death secretly filled me with triumph. It meant my father could no longer ignore me. He would need me as his partner in suffering and misfortune. For a few weeks I was devoted to him and put all my energies into proving myself worthy of his love. The colder his behaviour toward me and the more he rejected me or withdrew from me, the more unremitting I became in my attentions. Eventually, I felt so hopelessly disappointed, so frightened of the prospect of being finally and utterly alone in the world, that I hurled the very words at him that I knew must hurt and provoke him most. "Mama's death was all your fault!" I screamed, desperate to get through to him, desperate to provoke some feeling of guilt in him, or at least, if all else failed, to incur his wrath. It worked. Before I knew what was happening my father had leapt up from the table and grabbed me by the collar of my dress. His action and grip reminded me of when I once saw him catch a fleeing hen, slaughtering it on the tree stump next to the henhouse. The stone avalanche of his fists coming down on me was crueller than anything I had ever known. He kept on hitting me until he had murdered my last, faint hope that he would ever love me.

I lay on the attic floor, wrapped up in my mother's clothes, in uncanny proximity to my father who was sleeping two floors below and who, oddly, had done nothing to interfere with the freedom and depravity of my life spent roaming the streets. He didn't even protect his own flat against me. I robbed his larder as often as I dared, or as often as I managed to get into the house unnoticed, creeping in the semi-darkness past the windows that looked out onto the yard, round to the front door, which, as luck would have it, was often left open despite the rules laid down by the German caretaker. I not only stole my father's bread, his tins of sardines and the milk he drank with unswerving medicinal regularity every day after work, I also gradually began to remove my clothes, shoes and various other necessities, even misappropriating a blanket on one occasion, depositing it in my shed by the river for the cold nights I spent there.

I began to wonder whether my father hadn't changed his mind about me. Could he really have become kind-hearted and considerate at last? Had he really decided to give me my freedom after all? Wasn't it possible that he might even feel remorse? And was letting me get away with my current behaviour his way of making amends? Or was the opposite true, and he had only given me my freedom so that I could prove how thoroughly wicked I was? Was he simply waiting for the damning facts to pile up before him and supply him with enough evidence to justify his murdering me with a clear conscience? Or was he glad to be rid of me since I had never meant anything to him anyway? Perhaps he had given me up for lost, left me to a fate he considered hopeless, since in his eyes I was nothing but a useless remnant of my mother with no value of my own, a bothersome leftover that had only ever meant trouble and had finally left him in peace. Or had my disappearance freed him from someone who knew too much about his crimes against my mother, whom he had beaten and tortured just as he had me? Hadn't my disappearance finally released him from every last vestige of his past? After all, he had severed every other connection with his past life, with his origins, with Russia, with Germany, with his children and wives, with all the living and the dead, even with the very fact of his wife's suicide. And having cut himself off from everyone he had ever known and hated, for he despised all human beings, surely he'd be glad to be rid of me, the last human being in his life? Perhaps he derived a certain satisfaction from my homelessness, from knowing I was roaming the streets, drifting inexorably towards my doom. Perhaps this passivity of his was really a means of supporting my undoing. He was probably convinced that my ruin was inevitable, and that it was no longer necessary for him to do anything further to encourage it. Or was it pointless trying to dig down to the roots? Perhaps flight was a way of life in our family, a means of survival, and I was merely the next in line, the next link in a chain reaction that none of us could break because none of us knew the hidden recess of our common past in which it had all begun. Or was the real reason for his hatred his lust for "a young girl who was innocent in the true sense of the word"? Did he not get a vicarious pleasure out of leaving me to my fate on the streets? Wasn't it his lust for me that had always made him hate me? Hadn't his ill-treatment and chastisement of me always been a means of punishing himself? Was it not his own dirt which had defied all my efforts to clean the flat? Perhaps his obsession with cleanliness was the expression of a sexual mania which had transferred itself to me. Wasn't he letting me roam the streets because the kind of freedom that that gave me allowed him to feel that he had me where he wanted me? And wasn't my father now continuing his flight by running away from his own daughter?

There was no point in trying to dig down to the roots. There was no beginning. Only an end, the end of a process of which I was a part. It was an execution, and it felt like the execution of my father's will. For it seemed that the man I was soon to meet would merely be the executor of my father's will. He would simply be someone who picked up where my father left off.

On one occasion, a piercing scream wakes me. I start in

horror with no idea where I am or what has happened. Has someone discovered me? Have I been caught? Am I done for? Then I recognise the white of drying sheets in the dawn light. I'm in the attic and there's a woman standing in front of me. It's Marjanka, the Pole, with gaping eyes, her hand pressed firmly to her mouth: "I think you dead," she whispers. At last someone knows about my dreadful life. At last I exist, even if it's only as the cause of someone's dismay.

On another occasion, passing through the yard in the darkness, I bump into the Armenian. As usual, he's wandering about unable to sleep, the red dot of his glowing cigarette ghosting through the dark yard like the eye of some wounded, restless, nocturnal animal. This Muslim from an Armenian mountain village is driven by one obsession: the thought that he's given away his only son to the Germans, and that all the nights spent with his young wife will never give him back his son, and that his punishment each and every year is yet another daughter, whom he does love, but with a love that is really love for his son, since each new child is a substitute for the one child he has lost. And suddenly, I bump into him in the dark. How was I supposed to understand? All the adults I had ever met had turned out to be enemies, avenging angels whose sole business with me was retribution, whose superiority meant my survival depended on cunning and deceit, on the most extreme forms of resistance imaginable. How was I supposed to understand what the man meant? Terrified, I tried to escape, but all at once he had hold of my sleeve: "You no frightened! You father no good . . . You come live in my house." How was I supposed to understand this when the power of adults stood against me like a united front in which even Russia itself was in league with Germany; an indivisible unity in which even my father and Germany were one, and the Armenian naturally one with my father. Even German children belonged to the realm of adult power. Even they were part of this authority over me, part of the danger that constantly threatened me, against which my only defences were cunning and deceit, and my legs, which were faster than everyone else's because they had always had to be. How was I to understand that the Armenian was offering me something I had always searched for in vain: a house, a home, perhaps even a father. Perhaps this was his way of making up to a discarded, disowned child. I tore myself from him and fled, fled to the darkness down by the river where my shed was and where I could be alone, crawling under the blankets and into myself, into the protective shell of my body, which was getting smaller and smaller as time went by, becoming less and less habitable. For it was as if the hostile world had found inroads into my body, and as if there, too, my chances of finding warmth and a space for myself were running out fast.

I remember a departure, and two faces melting into one: Ida's on the platform in Brussels, and my mother's on the platform of the small German town where we lived. Two faces, weeping uncontrollably, in each of which I see my own. The train shudders and starts to move. The faces grow smaller. They disappear. Only my face is left.

Then a long gap, and Ida's face reappears, Ida coming over and holding out a bowl of milk to me. She has a bright, round face with light, rimless spectacles and thick brown curly hair. The room I'm in is big and dark and strange, more like a vault than a room. In the corner opposite me there's a weird monster made of dark, bottle-green tiles, and in the middle of the room, a big, roughly hewn wooden table with twelve different chairs, including some stools and armchairs. It's odd! They don't try to force me to do anything here. They let me cower on the floor in the corner all day long. They don't even try and persuade me. Only Ida comes over with a bowl of warm, fresh cow's milk, and when I don't want to drink it she puts it down beside me and goes away, as if I were a sick puppy. A little later, another girl comes over. She has strawberry-coloured cheeks and black curls and says something I can't understand. Then she puts down beside me a small yellow teddy bear with one eye missing. And after a little while, a big boy who's almost grown-up and whose curls are the colour of a swallow's nest comes over. Smiling awkwardly, he puts down a top and whip. By evening I'm surrounded in my corner by presents: chocolate, apples, toys, including a catapult made from a forked stick left by José whose curls are black as tar, and a big, reddish-yellow orange left by Carmen whose hair is like José's. It's the first time anyone has tried to win my affections, and I can't understand it. It's the first time people haven't tried to force me, and I just don't understand it. It's the first time anyone has ever waited for me and, at last, towards evening, when everyone's already eaten and the twelfth plate has been left untouched on the table, when I'm exhausted with hunger and crying, I pluck up courage and leave my corner. And then, under the gaze of eleven pairs of silent eyes, mother Evrard fills my plate again and again with roast meat, potatoes, vegetable nettles and dandelion salad.

I'm on a farm in Petit Thier, a little village in the French-speaking part of Belgium. It's one of the first years after the war and hungry children from the western part of Germany are being looked after by the neighbouring countries, probably as part of some Allied relief programme.

At first Belgium is just another Germany to me. It's a desert where no one can speak my language, where I can't understand what people are saying and nobody can understand me. I'm just the same person I always was, a person who can't speak. I'm deaf and dumb, just as I was when I first went to school in Germany. But there *is* something different here. I don't get chased after school. There's no teacher to humiliate me by making remarks about the Russians. Nobody here teases me or laughs at me. There are no punishments here like the ones I'm used to at home. There are no beatings. Everything I'm used to has suddenly gone. But I only notice the change gradually. It only dawns on me when I notice that the barrier of silence between me and the world has grown smaller. It's the second time this has happened to me, and my desperate desire to belong and be accepted makes it happen as rapidly now as it did the first time. But it's still a gradual process. And I only begin to notice the change when I realise I no longer feel quite as dreadfully homesick for my mother as I used to. I notice it in something else, too. When I've got over my language barrier, there's no new torture waiting for me on the other side, no new wall behind the first wall. And suddenly I no longer have to contend with things which I'd got so used to in Germany, I hadn't even realised that they were the cause of my unhappiness.

I've become the scourge of all eleven members of the family. From morning until night I do nothing but fight for my fair share of work, as if labouring in the fields and stables were my idea of heaven on earth. I want to do just as much work as mother and father Evrard's other children. I want to wade around in manure like they do. I want to harvest hay and potatoes like they do. I want to sit up on the tractor like they do. I want to milk the cows like they do (and eventually I'm allowed to pester Belle, whose brown coat has turned grey with age, tormenting her so much that even she, the patience of Job incarnate, decides she's had enough of me and kicks over a full bucket of milk). I want to help bake the bread and cakes like they do. I want to feed the calves and pigs like they do. I want to get up at four in the morning like they do, and I want to sit up in the evening in a room lit only by one weak bulb and darn socks like mother Evrard. And I want calluses and torn, bleeding skin like she has. Every twelfth evening it's my turn to decide what we're going to pray for when we say the Rosary before going to bed. And in fervent anticipation of the miracle I want to happen to my hair, I say: *Puisque les boucles croissent à Natalie.* I suffer from my lack of curly hair as if it's some new defect I've discovered in myself. Now that I've almost acquired the much coveted calluses and cuts in my skin, this defect is the last distinguishing feature which sets me apart from the other children in the family, making me as pale in their company as a lapwing among pheasants. But for a whole year, my lack of curls is the only thing that makes me Russian, the only thing that makes me different from the world around me, a world which has suddenly stopped opposing me. For a whole year I am almost happy. My happiness is broken only when a postcard from my mother arrives, telling me that everything has changed and that when I return home nothing will ever be the same again. And for the first time in this new environment of mine, I come across something I recognise only too well. They don't take me seriously. They don't believe me when I tell them what the postcard says. For the first time I'm all alone here with my fear. And the irony is that my mother's words are probably a cry for help, an appeal to this other world that is obviously so much better than ours because I write such happy letters home. Her words are probably her way of telling this world that she no longer has any room for her child.

But Belgium is also my first experience of a rupture, the shattering of a world which I took for granted. It is the first rupture between me and the paradise in which I had no identity. Because Belgium was paradise to me, and I could only identify it as such once I was expelled from it and had become aware of my own identity as a refugee.

I leave Ida behind me on the platform, her tears of sympathy mingling with my own tears of foreboding. And I say goodbye to Marie-Rose, Carmen, José, Paul, Lucien, Thérèse, Auguste and Claude, and to mother and father Evrard. I say goodbye to the life of these poor Belgian peasant farmers who have allowed me to be an ordinary child for the first time in my life. My mother stands waiting for me on the platform in

Germany, looking just like her postcard said she would. She looks almost the same as she will look four weeks later behind the glass panel in the chapel of rest. She just stands there like a statue. She doesn't even hug me.

The houses down by the millstream where Achim Uhland lived were a twofold source of mystery to me, for the mystery of Achim Uhland had merely intensified a sense of mystery which these houses had already held for me as a child. Today, these places have fallen into the hands of estate agents and property speculators. Sometimes given names like "Little Venice", they are lived in by people who can afford the extravagance of a romantic setting combined with modern conveniences. In those days, however, long before that kind of luxurious residence became fashionable, it was the poor side of town: a dark, narrow alley along a greeny-black mill-race which stank of sewage. The constant roaring of the stream filled the whole lane, interrupted only by the tormented groans of an old mill-wheel that turned its rotting scoops through the water day and night as if making a final, vain effort to keep going, although the mill itself was no longer in use. In the lee of the mossy, fortress-like walls of the mill, a row of crouched, half-timbered houses, interlocked like a series of crooked matchboxes, clutching one another along the bank of the stream as if trying to keep warm, or as if age had made them too weak to stand up on their own. They had small, fragile-looking balconies and doll's-house galleries which looked out over the stream and were adorned here and there with washing that was less likely to be drying than mouldering in the damp, subterranean air of the alleyway. A few drooping geraniums splashed lonely dots of red on the scene. These flowers were small and tired, like the balconies on which they grew, which themselves looked as if they might crash down into the stream at any moment. The houses were like wrinkled faces covered in scabs and eczema, the faces of ancient women, sitting along the bank of the stream like a row of grey hens. Germany actually meant something quite different from this, something new, immaculate and sparkling. And yet it seemed to me that the dark, secret interior of the Germany I was really looking for was here, among these cramped, crumbling walls. It wasn't only Achim Uhland who lived here. This alley held a third source of mystery for me: Christa. I had met Christa when I was hanging about here one day, as I often did, waiting for Achim Uhland. I'd spent days and nights waiting in vain, and then one day, Christa came along and took me home with her. Nothing like that had ever happened to me before. It was the first time any German girl had ever invited me home. I had long since given up hoping for a German girlfriend. I'd had to fall back on what was female in myself. I'd had nothing else to go on, only the things they had warned us about daily at the convent: the dark seductive powers of woman, powers that could ruin a man. I had decided I would have to rely on the worst in myself if I were ever going to acquire an entry ticket to the German world, to the world itself.

Christa was shrouded in the secret identity I had spun for myself, in the tales my mother had put into my head of a child whose true origins nobody knew. It was the legend of the foundling that made Christa's destiny seem tacitly interwoven with my own. Perhaps she didn't know herself who she was. With her black hair and aloof, feline timidity, she personified to me the story of a gypsy child who had fallen off a cart and was lost, or the story my mother had told me of Pharoah's child set adrift in a sewing box among the flags by the river.

She personified everything I saw in myself, the myth of all outcast children. But at the same time, she also personified everything I was not, a child who had been found, rescued, taken in. Like some bird of paradise who had forgotten how to sing, she lived with her German foster mother in a tiny, dark attic flat in one of the houses down by the stream. My oldest and deepest wish had come true for her. Like me she was different and foreign, but she had become the child of a German mother. It mattered not a jot that this German mother was an ugly old woman with twisted, arthritic joints, or that the dark, fusty old attic exuded nothing but misery and poverty; to me it was suffused in the brilliant light of salvation. In this mute and musty warmth there was a security I had never known, which my mother had been unable to give me because she herself was abandoned and foreign in this land. Only once, on the farm in Belgium, had I caught a glimpse of what it was to be cared for, to have my own place in the world, but that was long ago and long forgotten. If I remembered it at all, then only as one remembers the shreds of a distant dream.

From the very first day Christa took me in, her foster mother became the object of all my hopes. Whenever I came to her, often starving, my body's last reserves used up in the struggle to survive in the wilderness, she would place a plate of soup or stew before me as if there were some unspoken agreement between us. The body I have now, a body that has eaten its fill, makes it almost impossible for me to describe the hunger I knew then. Perhaps my only access to it is through the damage my body has suffered as a result, a body that still has to struggle from day to day even in the warmth and sated affluence of the world I live in now; a body full of faults and residual pockets of pain, which suffers regular collapses and only seems able to survive because I force it to. But especially at weekends, when I was ravenous and barred from plundering the larder in my father's flat, and all I could do was roam the fields beyond the river in search of something to eat, when my hunger had gone beyond its initial, strangely light-headed, euphoric stage and taken on an uncontrollable life of its own, becoming a creature inside me with the power to kill everything else in me, everything in me that was more than just a body, then the plates of soup or thick broth that Christa's foster mother set down before me gave me back a part of myself, a part of my soul, contained in the substance of potatoes and cabbage. This was the first German house I'd been allowed to set foot in and I would gladly have stayed if I'd been able to, like a stray dog who'd found a new home. If only I could have been this German foster mother's second child! But her dark attic room was scarcely large enough for herself and Christa, who had probably turned up like a stray dog herself. Each time I climbed the gloomy staircase for my food, I firmly believed that I was on the brink of salvation. I felt a miracle was about to happen. And hadn't it already, since I'd come to the attention of a German foster mother, had become a visible person to her? But even if I wasn't allowed to stay, the house by the millstream saved me again and again from the worst ravages of my hunger. Perhaps it even saved my life. This house by the millstream was the only real charity Germany ever showed me.

Achim Uhland's house was the last one in the row, where the stream plunged into a weir and its roar swelled to that of a raging torrent. This house was my only means of getting close to him, the only part of him I could see whenever I wanted. I could touch it and secretly imagine I was being touched by Achim Uhland. It seemed to me then that I had always been drawn to this lane because of Achim Uhland, as if this lane had meant Achim Uhland to me even as a child, and as if I had recognised this strangest of fairy-tale German streets in Achim Uhland from the very first.

He seldom comes here, and I rarely see him. Sometimes, under cover of darkness or dusk, which is thicker here than anywhere else in town, almost as thick as the darkness down by the river behind the "houses", I venture close enough to the house to let its cold cracked walls touch me. It's the only house here with no decoration of any kind, no balcony, no gallery, no skylight; simply four bare, crumbling walls and a grey roof which is losing its slates. I daren't stand for long at its low windows and peer through the threadbare net curtains, which are like dusty cobwebs, into a lit room, a kind of kitchen-cum-living room that somehow reminds me of a train station, a dingy waiting room on a station platform. I daren't stand here for more than a few minutes observing the man who lives in this room. Like some dangerous, brooding beast trapped in a cage, he sits there surrounded by beer bottles, and the atmosphere is so heavily charged, so thick with cigarette smoke, that each of his sluggish and yet unexpected movements is like a threat, a warning to anyone who has strayed too close to his house. It seems almost impossible to me that this man could be Achim Uhland's father, and yet I know that he is. I know far more about Achim Uhland than he could possibly surmise. This arcane knowledge is my most valuable possession. I inspect it daily, arranging it and rearranging it again and again in my mind, fully convinced that I only have to put its components together in the correct way for a picture of Achim Uhland's life to emerge in which I, too, have my place. But I have to pay dearly for each new addition to this jigsaw, whose ultimate function is to reveal the inevitability of my match with Achim Uhland. I have to pay the price of allowing Hans to take my hand and walk up and down the High Street with me as if he were my fiancé and were going to marry me. Hans is not only my only source of information about Achim Uhland, he is also my one and only contact with him. It is to Hans that I owe those few moments of dreamlike bliss standing next to Achim Uhland on the street. For occasionally he stops to talk to Hans when I'm out walking with him, or Hans, walking with Achim Uhland, stops to talk to me. And it sometimes happens on these occasions that Achim Uhland even exchanges a few words with me, giving me one of those looks that sets my hope on fire, making me feel certain that one day he'll see how right I am for him, and that one day I'll make him see how worthy I am of his love. That, after all, is my sole reason for living. All day and all night I comb the town for him. I wait for him down by the weir for days and nights on end, just to confirm to myself that he really exists. Hidden behind a wall I watch as he gets off his moped and goes inside, never staying long, reappearing a few minutes later before speeding off on his moped. And from the tiny shreds of evidence I tear from Hans in exchange for my two-faced company on our walks together, I gradually form a picture of Achim Uhland's life when he's not at the house by the weir. The only pieces of information I refuse to include in my jigsaw are his dates with Manuela, with whom I sometimes see him on the street, although I know Manuela means everything to him, just as he does to me. Achim Uhland's unrequited love for Manuela has become so frequent a topic of High Street gossip that it has even filtered through to me. Everyone in town seems to know about it, and sometimes I feel the tortured hopelessness of his love for her merge with my own, as if his love for another were not something keeping us apart, but yet another knot binding us, tied by the hand that determined the linking of our destinies in the primordial darkness of the world's beginning. I feel his torture as if it were my own, as if it were the same as the hell he's putting me through, a hell in which we are separate, and therefore one.

It's dark down by the weir, dark as a chasm with a cold, black waterfall, and I wait. I'm waiting for him, determined this time to come out from my hiding place behind the wall. Something extraordinary happened on the High Street today. I met him with Hans, and Hans, with whom I've never dared leave the safety of the busy town, tried to talk me into meeting him at the park this evening. Before Achim Uhland's very eyes, I'd become an object of desire, someone with the right to spurn another. Hans's pleading gaze courting my favour had turned my love into a desirable object which I offered Achim Uhland as my sole possession, punishing Hans with the same haughty condescension that I'd felt Achim Uhland direct towards myself. At the same time, I saw Hans as if I were looking at myself through Achim Uhland's eyes. I was an object of disdain, a spurned lover, an unsuccessful beggar who couldn't even hope to be given the time of day. But suddenly, Achim Uhland suggested I meet *him* instead of Hans in the park this evening. It had sounded unlikely from the start, and of course it wasn't Achim Uhland I found waiting in the park for me at the agreed time, but Hans. At first I thought that Hans, knowing I was bound to come to the park, had simply grabbed his chance and come along before Achim Uhland, taking me in his arms with the violence I'd always known was there in him, yet had always managed to escape. When Achim Uhland still didn't come, I thought he must just be late and would turn up at any minute and free me, since I could no longer free myself. But Hans had his arms around me, refusing to let go and was swearing he would kill himself if I didn't love him. I strained my limbs and tried to struggle free, pressing my teeth and lips together to avoid his mouth, which I loathed, but which I'd never repaid for all the information about Achim Uhland I had managed to extract from it. Then I thought Hans must be abusing a favour Achim Uhland had asked of him. Perhaps Achim Uhland had asked him to bring a message to me. Perhaps he had even asked him to take me to some new rendezvous. I suddenly realised I was in a trap. I'd always known this trap might snap shut and leave me in the hands I'd wronged by holding them so falsely on the High Street. Then I had the full weight of his body on top of me, pressing me down onto the park bench, and his hot panting breath in my face, and everything became less and less clear in my mind. I couldn't make out what was going on. I could feel that something was happening to the body on top of me, something I didn't know about, something that went beyond the tests I'd been put to at the hands of the German craftsmen. There was only the material of my clothes between me and the brutality of what was going on in this body which suddenly cried out in pain and collapsed on top of me in a soft, feeble heap. For a split second I'd seen a mutilated, distorted face above me, twitching as if it were made of some kind of red pastry, and then I was free and took to my heels.

I came straight to the weir and have waited here ever since. Now I've calmed down a bit, I tell myself it was probably all some kind of misunderstanding. Perhaps it was quite clear from the start that Hans was going to be waiting for me on the bench in the grotto, and not Achim Uhland. Perhaps everything was quite normal and that was just their way of going about things. Everything had worked out just as it was supposed to, and the only problem was that, as usual, I didn't understand what *was* normal, didn't understand the way German words and customs worked. Perhaps it was all just a test, and I was supposed to prove to Achim Uhland through Hans that I was worthy of marriage. Perhaps he already considered me his bride. Or perhaps the only reason he didn't was because I had been incapable of proving myself and because my background and low birth meant I would always be incapable, and because now Achim Uhland had all the proof he needed – proof that I was a "Russian slut".

The darkness of the lane had swallowed the house by the weir. The light in the window had long since gone out, submerging the man inside in darkness, too. Only the dirty yellow glimmer of a distant streetlamp brushed itself against the walls. The roar of the weir had become inseparable from the roaring inside my own skull, the roaring confusion of my brain. There was a musty, rancid smell like cat's urine, a smell that was somehow filling, making me want to breathe it in like some food, or like a poison for the hungry beast gnawing my insides, ripping the flesh from my bones. "Eight o'clock this evening at the bench in the grotto," was what he had said. I knew the German word for "eight". I knew the German word for "evening", the German word for "bench"; I knew all the other words in the sentence. But my problem was always that the German I was certain I knew could suddenly become very uncertain. I was always making a fool of myself. It wasn't the words themselves, it was what came with them, their aura. This was a veritable minefield for me, a maze, an invisible patch of ice I'd suddenly slip on and go ahead over heels to the derisive mirth of whatever company happened to be assembled. I could trust neither my ears nor my vocal chords. They were my constant pitfalls. They were always ambushing me when I least expected it. But I always forgot this, always forgot that my Russian ears simply couldn't hear German. They were incapable of deciphering German codes. And now this incapacity was the only hope I had left, this inability of my ears to hear what was between the lines, what was hidden behind and below the German words. This time I was clinging to the very thing that had plunged me so often into an abyss of humiliation and chaos. And it was as if I were clinging to a lifebuoy.

When he did show up it was already too late for me to make a dive for my usual hiding place behind the wall. I heard the buzz of the moped against the thunderous roar of the weir and the roaring of my own tired brain, but it didn't seem to mean anything to me. I was sitting, perhaps even sleeping, on the steps in front of his house, and by the time I realised what was happening and had sprung to my feet, he was standing right in front of me. His face was just a shadow in the dark and betrayed no surprise whatsoever, whereas I had probably revealed everything, my whole secret life spent in the shadow of his, a life in the thrall of my own yearning. I stammered out something I hardly understood myself, a jumble of sounds, but he just walked straight past me. Just as he reached the door, he turned his head in a deliberately casual manner, a movement which made the metal buttons on his leather jacket flash for a second in the dark: "What's up with you? I just felt sorry for him, that's all." And before I had grasped whom he'd felt sorry for, he was gone.

One cannot run away from oneself. "I" – that is the truth! . . . We spend our entire lives immured in the prison cells of our own personalities, and whenever the strength to be silent fails us, we talk about ourselves.

Anatole France

In a dream, a person I don't recognise hands me a plastic bag, like the type you get in supermarkets, and says: "There, this is your inheritance!" I take the bag and look inside it. It contains my parents' worn family album with its black-and-white striped plastic cover. Something tells me there is an invisible seal on this album and I won't be able to open it, although I know its contents off by heart already. Most of its pages are empty. The photos have obviously been removed from their corners, or else there weren't any there in the first place. The few photos one does come across are desert islands in a sea of blank pages . . . A pre-revolutionary photo of my mother's family, but without my mother. Just her father, a Ukrainian lawyer with an impressive imperial beard and a pince-nez hanging down onto the waistcoat he's wearing under his jacket. He is surrounded by women, probably aunts or cousins, wearing dresses like characters in a Chekhov play . . . A photo of my mother when she was very young, with her own mother, who was supposed to have been an Italian aristocrat, the daughter of an Italian textiles manufacturer with a factory in Kiev. With her white hair and severe, dignified features, she looks too old to have such a young daughter. Her shabby-looking dress with its white lace collar lends something of a departing *grandezza* to her sorely tried face. My mother can hardly have been much older than twenty in this photo. Her face reveals a staggering innocence which is almost impossible to reconcile with the knowledge it also betrays. The years of famine are clearly inscribed in this narrow face, with its pallid complexion and huge eyes. Her jet-black hair is bobbed and slightly wavy in a style that seems to combine something of both the fashion and the hardships of the times. Her shoulders are slender and graceful under her flowery summer dress, and even at that age, she had that same burning look in her eyes . . . On some of the other pages, a few "German photos" of my mother, my father and myself, awkwardly arranged for some street photographer or inside some pricey studio, my mother and I wearing the inevitable American CARE-package dresses . . . Two photos of me as a child. In both, I am all forehead drawn into a vertical, disgruntled frown, and rest of my face crumpled into a shapeless, concertinaed jumble of nose, mouth and chin, my thin hair hidden by an enormous, Russian, silk headscarf . . . A picture taken at my mother's grave shortly after her death, her brand-new gravestone set at the head of a freshly dug heap of earth and my father and I to the left and right of it standing at attention with forbiddingly solemn expressions on our faces, as if we were participating in some obligatory, military ritual . . . A picture of my Russian godmother, who died long ago, standing on the street in the pouring rain like some sodden piece of abandoned furniture . . . A postcard of Peter the Great wearing artisan clothing and flowing, shoulder-length curls, sitting on a stool against an unidentifiable background . . . An indoor shot of the shed that was our Russian church, with me, a dwarf clad all in Perlon, handing a bunch of flowers to a patriarch in a mitre . . . A few with faces I can hardly remember from my childhood, emigrés from other towns who sometimes came to visit us, among them Natalia Kirillovna with her white, smiling teeth and black curly hair, standing in the snow with a radiantly handsome Russian Mayakovsky-type before the portal of a German registry office . . . And Yulia Stepanovna, with her wax-coloured skin and heart condition, who died soon after my mother of her addiction to cigarettes and coffee and who was no older than my mother when she died . . . Loosely inserted between the pages are postcards showing my father's Russian émigré choir and my father in traditional Cossack dress. Also a number of Russian newspaper cuttings, mostly covering political events in the Soviet Union, and some postcards my father brought back from his tours: the beach on the German island of Norderney with its forest of canopied beach chairs, tulip fields in Holland, the Eiffel tower in France, a Spanish Flamenco dancer, the spa at Meran with its promenade a sea of oleander, and various other vistas of the big wide world which, in those days, seemed to exist only in legend. I also know there are two of my parents' documents in the album, their old work permits, issued in Leipzig on 8 August 1944. The photographs on these cards show my parents with numbers pinned to their breasts. The official seal of the Leipzig police headquarters is stamped at the top left and bottom right of each photo, bearing the Imperial eagle and a swastika. Under the photographs, next to their Russian signatures, are my parents' fingerprints, the right and left forefingers of each in the squares provided. "The holder of this permit is not Polish," it reads, and also: "This card is to be carried for purposes of identification at all times." My father's place of birth has been given a German name and distorted beyond all recognition. Under it:

Citizenship: undecided, eastern worker
Nationality: — —
Country of origin: Occupied eastern territories
Place of residence: — —
Occupation: Unskilled metalworker
Place of work: AGT. Maschinenbau GmbH,
Leipzig W 32, Schönauer Str. 101
Resident in Germany since 14. 5.1944
Then the official seal of the Leipzig Employment Office, also
with the Imperial eagle and a swastika.

A discreet item in a German daily newspaper, entitled
"Homesickness never lasts for ever. Ukrainian foreign workers
remember", has this to say about it: "Some of the survivors still
live among us today. Under the Nazi dictatorship during the
last war, over seven million foreign workers were deported to
Germany from 22 European countries. Most of them were
forced to work in munitions factories while others slaved in
the fields or in mines. The vast majority came from the Soviet
Union. They were seen everywhere in our towns and factories,
branded with the word EAST sewn onto their clothes. In Essen
and its environs alone some 400 camps were erected to house
this cheap labour. There is not one large company still
existing today, not one factory and hardly any small firm, that
did not apply to the Employment Office for "its" quota of
foreign workers. By the end of 1941 some five million foreign
workers had been deported to Germany and more than half
had died as a result of inhumane working and living
conditions. Our knowledge of this dark chapter in German
history still leaves much to be desired. It was forbidden to
photograph foreign workers and the death penalty threatened
anyone who spoke to them. The companies concerned refuse
to give information or to open their archives. Former foreign
workers who were unable to return home after the war are

often too ashamed to speak about their experiences, or prefer to forget."

The author Reinhard Laska was lucky enough to meet Andrei and Anna Lalatsch, who once worked on a farm in the Ukraine. They were prepared to talk about their past in front of a camera. Although they have lived in Germany for almost forty-five years, their language is still Ukrainian. Andrei Lalatsch tells his life-story in broken German, while their daughter has to act as an interpreter for Andrei's wife, Anna. Cut off from their roots, they are still officially referred to as "homeless aliens". They have no passports and no legal right to claim damages for the injustice they have suffered.

I might have been reading my own family history. Even the interpreting daughter fitted . . .

Finally, the album I'm dreaming about also contains a postcard my mother wrote to my father on 6. 10. 56, but never sent. It was written four days before she committed suicide:

> Dear Kolya,
> I have just sent you a parcel containing your winter coat, warm underclothes and woollen socks. Your wrist-watch is still being repaired. It's cold here in the mornings, so I'm sure you'll be glad of the warm things. Why haven't you written? Natashenka isn't very well. She has to stay in bed. I'll write a proper letter to you soon. With a kiss . . ."

She could hardly have written anything more trivial if she'd tried. Nothing could have sounded more innocuous! She writes this alibi for herself, diverts all suspicion from herself, and then doesn't even bother to take it to the postbox! The fact is, she doesn't need an alibi. The fact is that it doesn't make any difference anyway. Nobody cares about her. Least of all her husband! There's nobody to notice that her handwriting already says it all. It is the hand of someone about to disappear, the hand of someone already sinking, already falling. The lines slant off to the edge of the card, plunging away more and more steeply until, practically vertical, the writing becomes tiny, almost microscopic, and there's no space left for her name, so that she signs off with a little blob of ink in the bottom right-hand corner.

Apart from this album whose contents I already know, there are four ballpoint pens in the plastic bag. One of them is the kind I use; the other three are distinctly unpleasant. There's something menacing about them, something hostile. They look like instruments specially designed to torture the hand. In my dream I feel desperately disappointed by this pitiful inheritance. I wake up weeping like a child abandoned in the dark.

Later I ask myself why the album was sealed in the dream. Was it because it really was a closed book to me? Because I didn't really know what its contents were? Was it that its contents had never really been visible to me since I had only ever looked at them without actually seeing them, the way one looks at oneself in the mirror? And did the key to the magic seal on this book lie in the ballpoint pens I had been given with the album? Could writing utensils open the seal for me? Was writing the key to seeing, the key to unsealing the meaning of the pictures? Was that what the dream was trying to tell me? That the past was my possession, my inheritance, and writing the legacy this past had left me? If that were true, then the three unusable implements I had been given could only represent the impossible part of writing, the excruciating contortions one gets into, the convulsions, the tortures of the hand. They stood for the peculiar sense of deadlock writing involves, the experience that what one is writing is a failure and writing itself a continuous miscarriage. They stood for the fact that the heart of the matter, the thing one really wants to say, always remains unwritten, is always this blank space at the centre of what one is writing, and that however many words and sentences one adds, none of them ever gets to it, all are ultimately satellites orbiting a blank space. These writing utensils were crutches, which I had inherited. They were the crutches the cripple cannot do without, a necessary extension of his body, keeping him alive but also constantly reminding him he is a cripple. And perhaps he is a cripple only because he has discovered that there is no such thing as a reliable, supportive reality, nothing firm to hold on to, because he has discovered there *is* no reality. There is only his own, which doesn't exist either, so that the writer orbiting this reality is always a child abandoned in the dark, a child lost in a dark forest who never reaches the clearing, but who also can't stop searching for it.

It's as if this story I'm telling you – whoever *you* are, you, myself, perhaps something non-existent, the blank space I'm orbiting – were exactly the same as the story that really happened: a struggle with the inaccessible, with a sealed, self-contained world that refuses to let me in, always turning me back at its borders, a world that doesn't want me. The Germans who didn't want me are the words of this story. The words refuse to take this story in. They push it away as though frightened it might soil them. It's as though this story were too shameful for words, as though the words found it an impertinence, a form of harassment. The words constantly withdraw from me, and I constantly struggle with them. It's as if I were still dancing for my life in the German "Linden", still rattling at the nailed up window of my prison, still ringing my father's locked door, still rebounding from the contempt of the cold and beautiful German Achim Uhland, still being refused entry to the grace of the Catholic God, still shaking my petrified mother, who can no longer hear me, still in the dream where I had an iron head that couldn't break down the wall, the wall of this story that refuses to yield to my words. The person this story is about has no use for my words. She can't hear me. She can't understand me. I am someone who can speak, whereas she is someone who can't speak, someone who isn't in this story, who could only be there if language were not there; in other words, if this story were not there. Her German is a strangely disconcerting hotchpotch of local dialect, slang, her parents' Russianised German, the German babble of the "houses", the simple, cliché-ridden German of the Catholic nuns and the German she imagines a German society lady to speak. She doesn't understand the way I speak. To her I am inaccessible, unapproachable, incomprehensible. In short, German. Even in this story she is an alien, an outsider. She is the homeless outcast of this story. The more I say, the more homeless and outcast she becomes. No words can save her. There are no words that can accommodate her in this story, no words at all between her and me. She is the blank space I am orbiting. She is like you, a blank space that cannot hear, cannot speak, something I can no longer find in myself, as though it had been ripped out of me, aborted, drowned – like you. It's as though you were one person, she and you, as though you were conspiring against me and had decided not to come to my rescue because I didn't come to yours. You are she, and she is you, and I am an outsider in your story. I am roaming about in it like a stray beast. Homeless, hungry, freezing, I find nowhere to lay my head. For just as Adam and Eve could never have spoken of Paradise while they were still there, I could only tell my story once I had been expelled from it. But the real story will always remain untold, for the only language in which it could be told would be the lack of any language.

But what has happened
Should be covered with black cloth
And the lamps taken away . . . Night.

Anna Achmatova

It's easy to describe to you how it finally happened. One quick movement once we were inside the room – and he had locked the door. I saw the key vanish into his trouser pocket and before I knew it he had pushed me onto the bed next to the door. I didn't even have time to try and get back on my feet. He was on top of me straight away, twisting my arms. I screamed in pain and he shoved something into my mouth. I felt I was suffocating. Terrified, I spent the whole time after that, I don't know how long, just struggling to breathe. I hardly noticed the rest.

Why he didn't try and get it without using force I've no idea. After all, he had set it all up so nicely, just as men usually do when they're after a bit of cheap pleasure. He promised to marry me and take me back to Persia with him. He promised me I could live with him in the meantime in a big luxury flat. Evidently, he couldn't see any other way of getting me back to the shabbily furnished room he really lived in. But as soon as I'd crossed the threshold of his room, I wasn't really the kind of object he needed at all. To get to Persia I would have done anything in the world, anything he wanted me to. But he didn't want any risks, even if that meant giving up part of his pleasure. Who cared anyway about an under-age girl, who was obviously homeless, obviously on the look-out, who hung about in stations? He could be absolutely sure of getting away with it scot-free. Even if I had gone to the police, which was hardly likely in my case, they would never have believed me. Even he knew that, a foreigner, a Muslim. In fact he had better reason than most to know it. There was one thing he did get wrong, though. He must have taken me for German and probably thought he was raping a German girl. As a Persian, it was unlikely he could have got what he wanted from the body of a Slav.

One rainy night when I was in my shed, I thought I had finally found the answer. I had to get away before it was too late, away from this town. The town had brought me nothing but one calamity after another. It wasn't my salvation at all. It was just my father all over again. The town and my father were one. I had to get away to somewhere where nobody knew me, where nobody knew I was Russian or about the "houses", about my whole background. Luckily, I wore my background under my skin, visible only to those who knew. But everyone in this small town knew. And their knowledge was murdering me. Other people's knowledge had always been a curse on me.

The next day I locked myself in a train toilet. How surprised I was to arrive in the big city thirty miles away! I hadn't been there since I was a child. It had been a Sunday, the last time I had gone with my father and mother to mass in the shed that was our Russian church. I'd had an empty stomach, which in those days had given me that special, holy feeling you were meant to have when you received the Sacrament! I re-membered the trams, enormous streets that were utterly strange to me, shop windows with their glittering displays.

And as soon as I got off the platform, a miracle happened! He came straight up and spoke to me: a man in an elegant hound's-tooth check jacket. He said he was a Persian medicine student. He was much older than I was, much too old to be a student. He said he was rich, the son of the richest carpet manufacturer in Persia. And then he started telling me all kinds of things. We were going to get married, he said, and live in Teheran in his father's palace. He was a prince from the Arabian Nights. He was my salvation.

It wasn't until I got into the staircase of his house, which was in a street full of drab, post-war blocks somewhere near the station, that a peculiar feeling came over me. I went up a dirty, seedy-looking staircase whose sole sign of luxury was the penetrating smell of perfume coming from the man next to me himself, when suddenly, somewhere deep inside me, it all became quite clear. I brushed it aside, whatever it was, a false, superstitious voice in me that merely wanted to ruin this wonderful feeling of happiness.

I didn't know how long I'd been sitting on the floor. I was sitting behind a dark mountain of furniture. All I knew was that I could breathe again. I remembered having the same feeling as a child, and the fear had never left me. Perhaps it started when I had pneumonia: just this crack with me inside it, closing, pressing me out, squeezing me out of my body, and I'm desperately gasping for air, struggling to stay inside myself, and then, suddenly, the tunnel, already black, rips open. Suddenly there is air again. I breathed. I sat on the floor and breathed. But it wasn't over yet, I was still in the crack and it could close again at any moment. Somewhere behind the furniture the man was snoring on his bed. The only air was the air he was granting me by being asleep and snoring. I breathed in the man's perfumed air and knew that I had only to move for the air to turn into the man himself, into his perfumed hands, his perfumed body forcing me back into the crack. It was only now that I thought I could feel the man's movements inside me. It felt like a chisel pounding into me, while my arms were twisted behind my back, clamped into a system of pulleys that was tearing them apart at the joints. There was a burning feeling in my lower abdomen as if something inside me there were scorched. Carefully, without making a sound, I touched the pain. My fingers entered a soapy wetness that ran down onto my thighs, a wetness in which you had perhaps already struck root, but deeper inside me. He had torn my dress and my knickers. I had lost my shoes. They were lying somewhere in the darkness. I knew the door was locked. Now this room was the crack in which I hardly dared breathe. But I had to try and escape. As carefully as I could, holding my breath, listening at every moment I made, I felt my way forward through an unknown jungle of dark, closely packed furniture. The room was small and cramped, like a cage. Suddenly I knocked against the edge of something. I froze, terrified. The snoring faltered for a second, and then returned to its regular rhythm. I was standing right next to him. Almost at the door. The weak streetlight from the window fell on the blurred shape of his body. He was lying on the bed half turned to the wall, posing like some beast of prey, lithe as a beautiful wildcat stretching out its perfumed limbs, and for a few minutes the thundering of the blood in my temples drowned out the fretful sound of his snoring. I saw he was sleeping in his trousers. They had slipped half over his hips. His white shirt shimmered like snow in the darkness. I stretched out past him to the doorhandle which gave way noiselessly to the pressure of my hand – noiselessly and uselessly, merely proving the door was locked. It suddenly seemed important to find my shoes, as if they could help me get away, or as if they could give me back something of myself, some part of my body that had gone missing. I didn't dare try to feel for the key in the man's pocket. I couldn't risk waking him. There was a thick curtain drawn across the window which only just let in some light from a street-lamp outside and, for a moment, I imagined myself jumping, no matter how high the window nor how far to the street. For a moment I imagined myself screaming out into the street. In a rush of wild hope I saw myself screaming for help, but the scream stuck in my throat like a knife. It stayed there, stuck, because I knew there would be no help. Only a real knife could help me now, or the scissors I hadn't plunged into my father's back because he had got off me just in time. Now I knew what I had escaped from then. My body had experienced it before me, and I had not escaped this time. I had not escaped the fate marked out for the daughter of my father, the fate he had marked out on her body. I had not escaped this man who just happened to be the one to finish off what my father had begun.

I was sitting on the floor behind the furniture again. I had no idea how long I'd been sitting there. I was in the corner of the room furthest away from the bed with the snoring man, my head pressed under the protruding edge of a wash-basin. Now that my eyes had grown used to the dark, I managed to pick out my shoes on the floor. One of them was next to the man's bed. The other was lying between the bed and the corner of the room, where I had crawled the first time. And it really did feel like getting back part of myself from the man! Returning the shoes to my naked feet actually did make me feel safer! If only it would get light! If only the house and the street could come back to life, then, so I told myself, I'd be saved! But until then I had to avoid disturbing the snoring man at all costs. I had to prevent myself moving, had to prevent myself making even the slightest sound. I pressed myself into the corner as tightly as I could, trying to stop my body shivering with cold, trying not to think of the dreadful thirst that was cruelly exacerbated by my touching the wash-basin, a thirst I could only relieve by making a noise. And more than anything else I had to avoid thinking of the locked door. Somehow I had to suppress this knowledge, make it disappear in the darkness before panic made me lose my head. The knowledge was like a fuse burning inside me, like a flame coming ever closer, as if that other room were coming closer with it, the room with the locked door and nailed down window from which I had never really escaped. And from then on every door closing behind me would conjure up the same nightmarish vision of being trapped, whether lift doors, cinema doors, or tram doors. From then on every closing door turned me back into the suffocating, helpless prisoner I once was.

The wet, slimy stuff had dried on my legs and a sharp, unfamiliar stench, mingled with the smell of the man's perfume, rose from between my thighs and sent tremors of nausea through my body. It was hot in the room. The sultry August heat felt as if it must have been collecting in this room for days, or even weeks. It was as though the window had been closed for a long time in preparation for this very night, or as though the man had never opened the window in this room at all, in order to simulate an Asian climate. The material of my dress stuck to me like damp, warm seaweed, and there was nothing I could do to stop the shivering that seemed to be coming from some invisible, external organ of my body, or from somewhere deep inside me, from the core of my coldness, exhaustion and fear. Perhaps the morning had already begun outside. Perhaps there was only the thick curtain between me and the dawn light. But not a sound reached me from the street except for occasional passing cars which momentarily drowned out the man's snoring, which was growing weaker now and less regular. The sound of him sleeping was like a thin thread that could break at any moment, but although I could feel the danger growing, I couldn't keep my eyes open. Exhaustion plunged me into a world of black, thick spiders legs that were like levers, like the levers of machines, like a mad rush of levers, spokes and pistons all around me until I started in panic, immediately realising that the reality of my situation was far worse than the dream. Then I dreamed my dream of the prince who was still going to take me back to his father's palace in Persia, and only death could have stopped me going to live with him in a land that was so far from here, so different.

He woke up in the grey light and immediately raped me again. He didn't have to use so much force the second time. Then, putting his hand in his pocket, he produced a five-mark piece and held it out to me between the tips of his forefinger and thumb with the air of some graciously condescending benefactor. "For the journey home," said the man who, that night, had become your father.

How often I had wished my father dead! I had imagined myself murdering him, luring him to the river and pushing him in, poisoning him, stabbing him. I had imagined him as an ailing, paralytic old man who was dependent upon me for better or worse. The very thought of him weak and helpless and in my power gave me the strength to stay alive.

Now, I visit him two or three times a month in the sick ward of an old people's home. He is paralytic, he is ailing, he is old, and, for better or worse, he is dependent upon those who look after him. To kill him now, it would only be necessary to forget about him for a few days, just as he once forgot about me. One blow of the kind his fists once gave me dozens of would extinguish his life there and then. It would be enough to deprive him of his medicines – he wouldn't survive a day. But nobody does him the favour. No one is prepared to release him from the martyrdom of a body whose life is utterly exhausted, bereft of almost any redeeming human feature. No one relieves him of what is left of his unnaturally long life. For all that is left of him now is a dotard whose biblical longevity has finally grown obscene. It's as though death were the ultimate human weakness and as though its liberating power were denied to this man who had always despised human weakness, condemning him to suffer his own weakness to the very end. And he must have been so dreadfully weak all his life. For isn't all brutality a sign of weakness? There seems to be some kind of curse holding him back in this life, like that which makes criminals return to the scene of the crime. Perhaps his guilt has damned him to this inhuman longevity, sentencing him to live out the years my mother could have lived had she died a natural death, a punishment for the years she was deprived of. He has already survived her by three decades and was practically an old man when she died. A century seems terribly short when I see the better part of it compressed into this shrunken, wasted body which life has made so hard, it can't even lie down and die.

The old people's home is a huge concrete block with six floors and belongs to the Protestant Church. It is situated in a typical post-war housing estate with street names that conjure up Germany's lost eastern regions: *Breslauer Straße, Königs-berger Straße, Stettiner Straße*. The glass doors at the entrance are always decorated to remind visitors what season it is: Easter, Shrovetide, Thanksgiving, Advent. Everything is modern and gleaming. Everything is spick and span. All the rooms have hot and cold running water and most have their own balcony. There's a bar in the cellar, a gymnasium, a chapel. Two or three times a year, a lecture and slide show or a folk concert is held in the dining room. The more sprightly residents of the home have their breakfast and lunch in this dining room every day, taking sandwiches up to their room in the evening. There are dining areas on some of the floors for residents in so-called "part-care" who can't get down to the dining room. Residents confined to their beds are fed in their rooms. At the very top of the building, on the sixth floor, there is a so-called "closed ward" to accommodate advanced cases of sclerosis and senility.

My father has lived on the third floor of this place for almost fifteen years. He has his own room here and his own balcony. It is the first time he has ever lived among Germans. To begin with he was a stony-faced guest. Now he's a heap of rubble in what is known here as "full-time care". Incapable of looking after himself or keeping his room tidy, he has fallen into a state of neglect. Why this has to cost as much as a room in a luxury hotel on the Riviera is absolutely beyond me! Breakfast consists of two rolls with butter and jam. Lunch is watery soup, followed by a tiny piece of meat with potatoes and a few lettuce leaves. His evening meal consists of a couple of slices of cheap cheese or cold meat, a pickled gherkin and – straight from the butter-mountain – a cube of low-quality butter which has usually exceeded its expiry date. Those who can still get about go to the supermarket half an hour's walk away and buy themselves extra food out of what's left of their pension money, or from the 150 marks social security money they get every month, which is supposed to cover everything except their meals at the home. Apart from anything else, they need this money to tip the staff. They need it to get into the good books of the nurse who has to feed and change them all and generally get them ready for bed – all in two hours; or to bribe the nurse who has to do night duty on his own for all six floors of the home. Those who are incapable of doing anything for themselves, or only very little, those who have to creep about the corridors on crutches, or in walking-frames and wheel-chairs, in other words those who no longer have themselves, have nobody. They are like production components passing through a machine that oils and cleans them three times a day, if they're lucky. Their faces are expressionless. Their bodies, often hardly more than torsos, have somehow managed to miss their appointments with death. Instead, their lives have been taken over by a fully automated medical system so that they probably feel they have ended up in hell. The living rarely pay a visit to this place and I am never sure what those who still have their eyesight actually see in me when I come here. The liveliest among them beg for money to buy cigarettes and alcohol. Others raise their arms and threaten me: the only language a body condemned to this hell on earth has left. There are some who see the visitor from the outside world as their last hope of escape, demanding to be taken to the nearest station or bus stop, or to some other potential vanishing point. There are some for whom the guest from the outside world is the last person to witness how forsaken they are, the last person to witness the miserable end of a life the world has forgotten. There are those who see everyone around them as thieves and murderers, as villains and ruffians who hide their belongings and the keys to their cupboards, smear slippery soaps on their fragile possessions and put poison in their food. There are those whose life consists solely of quarrels with the other residents and petty-minded back-biting in the day-to-day struggle for preferential treatment by the nurses. And then there are the absent majority, ghosts, no longer really alive, one of whom is my father.

I don't know whether he really wants me to visit him, whether he even notices. He just sits there in his armchair, padded with cushions and nappies. He is small, grey and withdrawn into some bleak internal landscape where moraine nudges slowly through his ruined arteries and where he seems to be listening to the endless trickle of time. A thick layer of dust covers the furniture in his room, and the drainpipe of his wash-basin is infested with generations of bugs that are immune to all poisons. The curtains obviously haven't been washed for some time. The carpet is filthy and the room stinks of rotting bits of food nobody clears away and nappies nobody comes to change. Yet another ironic twist of fate! My father's first and last German domicile must make the fanaticism with which he once preached German cleanliness seem like a total delusion to him now. He has probably never had to live in so much dirt as in this German house; only here he is powerless to do anything about it. For nobody comes to see how he is. He's a so-called "borderline case", a resident who is not confined to his bed even though he may be weak and even quite helpless. The social welfare office pays for a nurse who doesn't seem to exist, a cleaner who doesn't clean and board and lodging that would be better in any third-class hotel and cost a third of the price to boot. The director of the home announces something over the loudspeakers out in the corridor: "For what we are about to receive, may the Lord make us truly thankful! Amen. Enjoy your meal!" But the evening meal was cleared away on this ward over half an hour ago . . .

I bring my father anything I know he's fond of and his rotten teeth are still capable of chewing: hot, spicy foods, a little bit of sheep's cheese, a morsel of smoked fish. His guts never retain what he eats. It goes straight through him while he's eating and comes out as a watery, greyish-yellow slime. He hasn't got used to a German diet even after fifteen years in this home, and his German hasn't improved since he first came to Germany. He continues to be sent his Russian newspapers and magazines, but almost blind now, he can no longer read them. Although his days consist of nothing more than the few chores necessary to survival at the most basic level, each of these days seems to demand a superhuman effort from him. He sits in his armchair for hours on end and shows no sign of boredom ever. It is as though there were events of enormous magnitude going on inside him, like the geological processes deep down in an ancient, overworked mine. He often seems to me to be entirely preoccupied with his internal bodily sounds. Occasionally he asks me what day it is, or what the weather is like outside, or whether my winter coat is new. I ask him about his various illnesses, about the gangrene threatening his leg, about his insomnia. I ask him whether he's in pain, or whether there's anything I can bring him. His desolate state reminds me of how I felt when he abandoned me, a loneliness as big and grey as the ocean. I suffer with him, so much so that it wakes me up at night. My sympathy eats away at me like acid. It suddenly grips me like a fever, and I even share his symptoms: asphyxia, attacks of dizziness and paralysis of the vocal chords. However far away I am from him, I can do nothing to prevent my own bodily organs reacting seismographically to the pain he feels. It is as though I were his prisoner, one body with him at last, as though he had finally succeeded in subjecting me to his will and obliterating me. It is as though his weakness had finally achieved what his strength had failed to do.

I couldn't bear him being weaker than me. I couldn't bear the idea of his becoming my child, since it meant I could no longer be his. I did all I could to persevere against my spiralling weakness, for although this weakness made it possible for me to be his child again, or even to become his child for the first time, it had to be greater than his weakness, which in turn meant the ultimate weakness: death. Only my death could make him stronger than me, and make me his child. But because I didn't want to die, I returned to the fantasies I once had of his death. I imagined myself, pillow in hand, about to smother him. I wasn't killing him to see him suffer; on the contrary, I did it because I didn't want to see him suffer any more, because I didn't want to suffer with him myself any more. I killed him to free myself of the child I no longer wanted to be, the abandoned, neglected, homeless child. I lay in bed at night and fought with him, wrestling with him for dear life. It was as though his life were not merely that of a moth lying on its back in a bed of silver dust, but were still the life of my murderer. It was as though his death were sucking out my life's blood, as though I could only avoid witnessing his death by letting his death bleed me to death before he died.

Two men, half coffin-bearers, half sedan-bearers, carry him up the steps to my flat in a strange contraption: half throne, half wheelchair. He sits there gesticulating like a malicious dwarf, like the father in Kafka's "Judgement": half king, half sick old man.

When I leave the old people's home after one of my visits I always avoid using the lift. I take the stairs instead. It's my old fear of my father's will cutting through time and catching up with me, trapping me under his roof for ever. When I leave the home in the darkness – and I always have to conduct these visits under cover of darkness – abandoning my father to his loneliness, I find I am still running away from him.

The summer was over. I had left the city and come back to the small town, where life had resumed its familiar course. My body was nothing but skin and bone. My cough produced a continuous burning sensation in my chest and I was repeatedly plagued by curious attacks of nausea. I felt as if a heavy lump of dough were rising inside me, surging backwards and forwards between my guts and my brain, sucking my eyes ever deeper into some foggy, dirty grey region inside my head from which my perceptions of the world about me were becoming increasingly unclear. Occasionally my insides erupted without warning, spewing out hard, undigested chunks of turnip and raw potato – the last I could find on the fields, along with the smoked fish I had stolen from my father, whose kitchen cupboard I continued to raid with impunity. I had long since given up washing my clothes in the river. It was far too cold for that; and anyway, I was no longer interested in my appearance since there was nobody I wanted to please. I spent most of my time wandering about the meadows by the river, oblivious to the changes in temperature and weather which already heralded the first morning and evening frosts of late autumn. Whenever the weather was fine, as it sometimes is in October, I warmed myself greedily in the mild sunshine, seeking out dry patches of earth or warm stones, just as lizards do in their search for maximum exposure to heat and light. But when the rain set in, and I could no longer stand the cold damp of the shed or the mildew on my makeshift bed, I was forced to take to the streets again. There were hostile, knowing eyes everywhere. I skulked about in shopping arcades or under the eaves, huddled in a stiff old raincoat I had taken from my father's flat. I spent hours at a time in the Heka store on the High Street, where I locked myself in the toilet to get some rest. Or I hung about the display counters, although the only one that really attracted me was the sweet counter since that was the only one that sold food. The sales assistants there knew me and never let me out of their sight, but once, when the shop was full of customers and nobody was watching, I managed to steal something. For the first time ever, I had actually done what people had always accused me of! I had finally gone beyond the pale! "Show me a liar and I'll show you a thief," was what the German children had chimed when they pinned me down and searched me for things that had disappeared from the classroom or from someone's locker at the convent. It's true that I told the most whopping fibs, but I had never stolen anything from the Germans. "Gypsies are thieves," said the Germans, and "Russians are thieves", too; I wasn't Russian because I wasn't a thief. But now I was a Russian and a gypsy in one. With no idea what was in the cellophane bag I had stolen, I took to my heels, my loot pressed close to my pounding heart under my raincoat. While I was running, I recalled the incident with the salami. I couldn't remember how it had all begun. The only thing I could remember was suddenly finding myself encircled in the convent refectory. Anita, a fat-faced butcher's daughter with a pug-nose, came up to me with a menacing look in her eyes and insisted I repeat after her: "I'm a dirty Russian liar and a thief". I pressed my lips together, determined to stay silent even on pain of death. They kicked me, punched me, threatened me, but they couldn't get a sound out of me. Though my hatred of these girls knew no bounds, they were certainly shrewd little devils when it came to finding a means of humiliating me. For I wasn't only a dirty Russian liar and a thief, not only a Russian heathen and a heretic, I was also one of the few girls at the convent who had no contact with the outside world. For years we had known nothing but the taste of prison food. Greed was written all over our faces whenever the others were sent parcels from home, or when they came back from their weekends-out with sausages and cakes, or when they returned to the convent after the Christmas and summer holidays bringing not only the sinful fragrance of freedom, but also that of roast meats, pastries and chocolate. This was especially true of Anita, whose locker in the corridor was like a butcher's larder. Every breakfast and evening meal I would watch her with renewed hope as she cut herself thick slices from a leg of smoked ham, or spread her bread with mountains of dripping and liver sausage. But she seemed to begrudge her neighbours, of whom I was one, even the smells exuded by these delicacies. So I was astounded when she produced a whole salami as thick as her arm from behind her back, swinging it to and fro in front of my nose like someone teasing a cat with a dead mouse. I had only to repeat that sentence and the salami would be mine. I looked around me and saw faces full of scorn and prurient expectancy. They knew my game was up. It was obvious I couldn't resist the bait. "I'm a dirty Russian liar and a thief," I said, speaking as quickly as I could. Then I grabbed the salami and ran, though I was far from suspecting that I had walked into a double trap. The irreversibility of my plight only dawned on me once I had eaten the salami down to the last morsel. It was Friday. I had eaten meat! That was what they had wanted! My situation was hopeless. It was part of the unquestioned daily routine at the convent for all the pupils to take Communion together at early morning mass. Not to go would be tantamount to publicly admitting to a mortal sin, and that had never happened. Mortal sin only existed in theory at the convent, a potential danger that had never found its counterpart in practice. I had been the invisible exception to this rule, but now I was the visible one. If I stuck to the rules and went to Communion the following day with everyone else, I would be exposing myself to Anita and her gang as a desecrator of the Body of Christ. If I didn't go, I would immediately be unmasked as the first mortal sinner ever to set foot inside the convent. This had to happen to me, of course. After all, I'd been christened a misbeliever, and it had only been a decision to temper justice with mercy that had allowed me into this Catholic sanctuary in the first place. I spent that night like someone in a death cell. However, the Catholic Saviour took pity on me for the first and last time. In the deathly hush during consecration, just as the server's bell began to ring for the third time, I felt sick. Everything began to swim before my eyes and then suddenly disappeared like chalk rubbed off a blackboard. I came to my senses between two sisters who were dragging me back to my bed in the dormitory. I was permitted to get up again that afternoon to accompany all the others to our usual Saturday confession in the cathedral. From then on, I went back to being the invisible mortal sinner and desecrator. Only the father confessor knew that I had confessed to no more than a few venial, childish sins, just as I did every Saturday. I was temporarily saved – and was damned to eternity. But nobody knew that except me. My day-to-day survival had always been based on pretence and deception. I had always fabricated a place for myself among others by stealth. In that sense I had always been a thief.

With my hands shaking as if in delirium, I attacked the booty I had carried out from the department store. It consisted of sweet, soapy lumps which later reminded me of bones, of sweetly perfumed bones, bones for making soap. They also reminded me of the smell and sperm of the Persian. And it was sperm I spewed up afterwards in a veritable orgy of revulsion, as if the very well-head of spider's spawn had opened up inside me, and as if that well had always contained the sweet-smelling, boiling spume which now came gushing in fountains from my mouth and nose.

I remember once taking shelter from the rain and suddenly finding myself in the station restaurant, where the waitress brought the cocoa I had ordered without a second glance at me. It had all somehow happened without me, like one of those moonstruck sleepwalking expeditions I had undertaken to the roof of our house as a child. And just as a gust of cool air had once awakened me as I tried to climb out of the skylight onto the roof, this time it was the warm liquid in my stomach that woke me. I awoke to find myself a thief for the second time, only this time it was as if I had stolen in my sleep. There was no going back. I saw the dirty, blue and white checked tablecloth in front of me, the empty cup with its brown cocoa stains, and glancing quickly to the side with my eyes still lowered, I noticed one other thing – the door. But my flight was not to succeed. A few minutes later I was sitting amidst a horde of drunken men who had ransomed me from the waitress. She had intercepted me at the door and dragged me over to the counter by the sleeve, using one hand to hold me fast while dialling the police with the other. It was then that my rescuers had intervened. Swearing loudly and threatening blue murder, the waitress had eventually agreed to hand me over to the men, who had added my cocoa to their own bill. These German men in their mason's overalls had stopped me going to prison. It was a miracle! They drew me into their circle of smoke and noise, and out of sheer gratitude to them, I started to drink. They plied me with schnaps and beer, and then more schnaps, and the only thing I remembered later was that, finding their appreciation of me was becoming increasingly violent, I had given them to understand that I was the world-famous Russian ballerina Anna Pavlova, and that if they so cared, I could give them a performance of "The Dying Swan". They were obviously game for a laugh and greeted my suggestion with loud approval. "The Dying Swan" had been one of my star party-pieces as a child when people came to visit us in the storeyard shed where we used to live. My father had presented me as a child prodigy. When I was five or six, I could recite whole sections from Pushkin's poems off by heart and sing Russian folk songs and ballads. Later, I had accompanied myself on an old accordion that my father had bought or found for me somewhere, and which was so big I couldn't even see over the top of it. But the enthusiasm with which my audience would greet these performances had always reached its climax when I danced my version of "The Dying Swan" à la Anna Pavlova, a figure who, in the picture from the *Russkaya Mysly* newspaper was all sinuous limbs and white feather tutu. I would dance to an imaginary version of Tchaikovsky's music, which I had never heard, but thought must be full of the convulsive sobbing of the dying creature. And it was this other, hidden side of Russia that I wanted to show the German men. I wanted to show them the side of Russia that they didn't know. I wanted to reveal it to them through the language of my body, the only language I had for communicating something Russian to the Germans. I wanted to show them Tchaikovsky and Anna Pavlova, the hidden side of myself, a side I'd found in Russian poetry as a child, a powerful and beautiful side to me that didn't exist in the real world, a part of me with no language of its own, which had spoken through the Russian songs and poems that had suddenly made everyone adore me when I had recited them to my audience in the shed. Most of all, I liked to recite Lermontov:

> Amid the ocean's blue expanse
> A distant sail gleams, white, alone.
> What do you seek in foreign lands?
> What have you left, lone sail, at home?
>
> The yard strains, the mast creaks,
> Over playful crests a shrill wind blows.
> Alas, no fortune here you seek,
> Nor flee some happy past you've known.
>
> Golden sunbeams give their warmth,
> Beneath lie clear blue seas,
> yet stubbornly, you pray for storms,
> as though storms harboured peace.

I couldn't recite this poem to the German men. Nor could I recite Pushkin's "Enchanted Bay" or Fyodor Glinka's "Prisoner's Song". But all these things were encompassed in my mind's eye by the dying figure of Anna Pavlova, by the imaginary Tchaikovsky resounding in my ears, by the wild agony of the swan and the language of its dying body which sent me tossing about the station restaurant in a sea of alcohol before the eyes of these German men, my course set firmly for the rocks of ridicule, for the climax of my striptease before them. Borrowing the name of a legendary, world-famous Russian star, who would naturally be entirely unknown to these German men in their mason's overalls, and with my imaginary wings beating in the final throes of death, I was once again offering the Germans my utmost, offering them my self in its most extreme form. I was offering them a combination which had always proved my peculiar biological catastrophe, the combination of the Russian and the female. I always made the same fatal error, hoping this combination would make people appreciate the Russian in me more. But the effect of this was merely to double the intensity of what German men saw in me as Russian.

Later, the prospect of survival seemed dependent on my amputating either the female in me or the Russian. I had to sever the fatal bond between the two. But since they were inseparably interwoven, I had to amputate both. I called this my attempt to be born dead, and the place where I felt most at home in this state was among the ghostly figures in black clothes who sit on doorsteps in Calabrian villages, beings without age or gender who have been dead a thousand years and who sit there as if they were part of the architecture, always knitting the same stocking as if it were eternity itself. It was here that I brought my experiment to a successful conclusion. I was as dead as it is possible to be with a living body, the only kind of death that life allows, the only possible human experience of nothingness which cannot be experienced after death. It was here that I found my Italian mental disease, which was also my mother's. Perhaps she had danced, too, long before I got to know her. Perhaps all these women had danced once. And look at me! I'm dancing again, too! I'm doing a striptease in front of you so that you will save me, so that you will save the world, so that you will remember there was once a time when your racism went so far that you turned human beings into lampshades and soap.

I only just managed to escape a second rape in the German station restaurant. It was the waitress who prevented the worst, who eventually rescued me and threw me out, swearing fire and brimstone and renewing her threats to call the police. And what if she hadn't rescued me? What difference would it have made? What's done is done and cannot be undone, and I was more than done for. Luckily for me though I was living in the dark. Luckily for me I had become darkness itself. I was so much in the dark that I even considered what had happened in the station restaurant to be normal, even felt gratitude for being saved twice, first by the men and then by the waitress. I had long since lost any notion of what was normal, and had never really possessed such a notion in the first place. I was like the little American boy who was locked up in a crate for two years and who was astonished when he was freed to find that all little boys didn't have to live in crates . . . Perhaps it was quite normal for my father to have locked me up. Perhaps the thing that the Persian did to me was quite normal, too, and what was really abnormal was myself and the way I continually doubted what was normal. In fact, one could hardly even call it doubt; it was just that I continuously experienced normality as a mortal threat, as humiliation. Of course my father, the Persian man and the German men in the station restaurant were normal! It was only my mother and myself who were not normal. It was this ineradicable, deadly nausea inside me that wasn't normal, this smell of perfume that never left me, overwhelming me when I was least expecting it so that I'd be sick again and again, bringing up a boiling, perfumed froth, bringing up the Persian over and over again. The image of the Persian in my mind mingled with that of my father, merged with the image of my father's quinine-coloured muscles twitching in the yellow cone of light in the room, an image from which my screaming mother's arms had wrenched me into darkness. Perhaps I had never left that darkness. Perhaps the darkness had even grown inside me, had already forced me out of the only territory I had left, the territory of my own body, in which I hadn't even noticed the presence of a second living being. I didn't even notice you when you were as big as an octopus and had been living inside me for five months, taking my own place inside the bag of skin and bones that was me, already easily visible to anyone who wanted to see you, invisible only to myself.

Occasionally, when nothing better occurred to me – and it became increasingly rare that anything much did occur to me – I would shelter from the rain in the church on the market-place. It was just as cold in there as it was outside, if not colder, but at least it was dry. Luckily there were often candles burning in the altar niches where I could warm my hands, and I could also sit in the pews and rest. Hanging under the great hollow dome above me was a huge cross on which the German Christ stretched out his crucified arms to receive the world into his suffering. I hadn't been to Catholic mass since my father had picked me up from the convent. I had sworn a solemn oath there to stay a Catholic and to go forth into the world of misbelievers and sow the seed of the one true belief. I was instructed by Sister M. that God had called upon this seed to bear its fruit in me for a higher purpose that would transcend the limits of my being. But entering the world of misbelievers at my father's side, this oath had accompanied me no further than a few hundred yards into the freedom beyond the convent gate. I had walked down the cobbled street of Cathedral Hill and felt my Catholic belief dwindle with each step I put between myself and my gloomy prison walls. It was as if my belief had been biding its time inside me all these years only to evaporate into thin air as soon as it was exposed to a free ray of sunlight. I left – and the profanity of the air that greeted me outside immediately changed me back into the heathen I had been on first entering the convent. I left with the incredulity of someone released from a life sentence who cannot grasp that she is really free. I wouldn't have been able to stop running in my newly found freedom had I not been disciplined by the regular pace of my father who was walking beside me in his coat and hat, carrying my suitcase, while I carried a cardboard box with the rest of my belongings on a string that squashed my fingers together . . . I remembered these things while I sat in the church on the market-place, fleeing from the wrath of the heavens under which I could find no shelter. And as I regarded the crucified Christ above me, I remembered another such Christ, my first encounter with him.

During one of our secret expeditions to the German areas that lay behind the "houses", Farida and I had come across a chapel. We didn't know what to think of the light-blue, stone building, shaped like a pavilion, and on trying the door were surprised to find it unlocked. There seemed to be nobody there, so we cautiously stepped into the bluish, almost crepuscular light inside. We spent a long time just staring in amazement at the strange, sumptuously decorated interior while it dawned on us that we were standing in a German place of worship. Full of devotion, we ran our fingers over the elaborate ornamentation of the pews, dipped them into the sweetish, mouldy-smelling water of the font, stroked the golden hem of the Madonna's garment and touched the starched lace of the altar cloth. Then, letting my curiosity and courage get the better of me, I put my finger on the bleeding wound on the foot of the crucified Christ that was hanging over the altar, as if touching it in this way might reveal to me the secret of the Germans. Shocked by my own audacity, I immediately withdrew my hand, only to discover to my disappointment that my finger had remained white and dry. I began to feel a sullen resentment against this German Christ, against this impostor who was cold and silent and indifferent towards me. Hoping to get some reaction out of him, I gave him a little punch on his naked shin bone. Farida followed suit, and the crucified figure swayed a little, high and lonely above us. But when we still weren't punished, and our hands neither fell off nor were turned into burning stigmata, we began to lose our tempers with this German Christ who refused to respond to us. We began to swear at him in German, Russian and Caucasian, using all the words we could think of. We began to spit at him and hit him more and more furiously. I saw Farida's face burn with destructive frenzy, and I knew it was the mirror-image of my own diabolical features. Tearing the flowers from the vase at the foot of the cross, we flung them with their wet, half-rotten stems at the helpless face of this German object of reverence, which was soon soaked from head to foot and covered in bits of dung-coloured muck. "Pig!" we screamed. "*Kurva*! You think you're a God, do you? You're nothing! *Pitschka materi*!" We cursed him with the names of our teachers, our mothers and fathers, with the names of all the authorities we hated, all the powers that stood over us. He was the first helpless German we had ever had at our mercy, and we rushed outside for new ammunition to fuel our orgy of revenge, ripping handfuls of grass from the earth and arming ourselves with stones. We raged and fumed until the power and holiness of the shrine were utterly desecrated, devastated, smashed to pieces. The only part of the Roman Catholic Christ left hanging on its cross was a torso covered in filth, while the rest of it lay scattered everywhere in earthen shards. Eventually, we realised the extent of the damage we had done, and coming back sharply to our senses, we took to our heels. We fled through the fields, swimming through yellow seas of ripe corn, panting from fear of our imaginary pursuers, convinced that some terrible nemesis awaited us ... That was how my relationship with the German, Catholic Christ had begun, and that was how it continued at the convent. I lived in daily expectation of my execution. And although I was still waiting, although the earthly fortress of the German Christ itself had released me without punishment, and although the same Christ was now permitting me to shelter from the bad weather under the dome of his church on the market-place, none of these things proved that I had been forgiven. They were no different from the mute, invisible presence with which my father had continued to abandon me to my freedom, to a strange freedom from punishment which seemed increasingly likely to end with the imposition of the maximum sentence the longer my impunity lasted.

It was still raining outside. I had no idea how long I had been sitting in the empty gloom of the church. Had I been asleep? Perhaps I had simply passed out from exhaustion. A strangely malignant, piercing cold had got inside me, so that even the rain now felt warm on my skin. I couldn't tell whether it was the rainy sky that made it so dark out on the street, or whether evening was already falling. I tried to remember when this day had begun, how it had begun, but there was only the mass of grey dough rising in my head, which seemed to rise out of the darkness of the street itself, out of the darkness of some beginning I could no longer remember. The mill-race, too, where I was suddenly startled by the squeaking and banging of the mill-wheel, was part of a beginning that had vanished from my memory, forced down behind my pupils into a foggy expanse full of hot little waves, tiny spouting geysers whose heat sent icy shudders through my body. I saw the dwarflike window of Christa's garret flat overlooking the street, or not so much overlooking as looking inwards, into an interior that had become too small for my hunger. Taking my familiar path along the mill-race, I saw that the stream was almost flooding its stone banks after the heavy rainfall of the last few days. The water had thickened to a bubbling, steel-grey syrup, so that the grinding buckets of the

mill-wheel looked like teeth that were about to get stuck in it
and break. It was like hot sludge that had reached boiling
point and was crying out for more and more rain, thirstily and
yet invisibly gulping down the water that poured from the sky
as soon as it touched the surface. There was something hostile
that emanated from this seething, straining torrent. It was the
cold heat of my own body, a viscous cold that was like molten
lead surging through my blood, parching my sodden body
with a dry thirst. Even from a distance I saw that the moped I
had come to know so well was not in its usual place in front of
the house at the weir. I saw that it really was dark, since the
electric lights were on in the two ground-floor windows of the
house. It looked even more frail and unstable than usual in
the pouring rain, indistinguishable in its hoary, tortoise-shell
colour from the town wall against which it leant. Only by
huddling up against the thousand year-old ruin of the wall
behind it did it seem capable of staying upright at all. It was a
rotting, invalid body, exhaling putrescence from the cuts and
gashes in its skin of peeling plaster. Through the window I
saw the man who was Achim Uhland's father. I saw his fearful,
gorilla-like body in its usual devastated environment, surrounded by empty beer bottles, apparently sleeping beside
the stove on a settee that was much too small for the body
lying on it. Despite the roar of the weir, I thought I could even
hear a snoring noise through the glass pane. I regarded him
with held breath, as though the sound of my own breathing
might wake him through the glass, and as though something
terrible were bound to happen if he were suddenly to move,
wake up with a start and notice me. I saw him gasp for breath
in his sleep. The air seemed to resist his attempts to inhale.
The air was an enemy which his body fought with violent,
convulsive stabs. There were long periods in which he
seemed not to breathe at all, in which the stranglehold at his

angular throat seemed to have throttled the life out of him, so that a watery thread of mucus ran out of the corner of his mouth and seeped into the copper stubble on his fleshy cheek. I saw the ginger hair on his puffy hand, which hung limply down from the settee, touching one of the spilt beer bottles, a hand that looked soft and spongy, but which probably concealed an immense concentration of force. His shirt had slipped out of the waistband of his disgusting, half-open trousers, and the podgy white flesh of his legs was visible between the hems of his rolled-up trouser legs and the tops of his socks. Another sudden jolt went through his body as he strained between two breaths. Like a landed fish trying to throw itself back into the water, his body reared up to get at the oxygen, arching as though pressing up against a stone lid, and then slumped again, apparently caving in under the enormous pressure of its own snoring, whose sound, drowned out by the roaring weir, I could only surmise. It was as though his body were bigger and more powerful than the building that housed it, so that the next breath that came from its massive hulk would send such a tremor through the weak, crumbling walls of the house that they would collapse on top of him. There was no room here for a second person. The colossus on the other side of this window needed the whole space for himself. In appearance, he was nothing like my father. On the contrary, he was the opposite of my father. Nevertheless, Achim Uhland and I had the nameless, impalpable violence of our fathers in common. The shadowy threat that emanated from this sleeping body might have been the menacing aura of my own father, with the sole exception that my father's muscles were taut as wire and steel and never missed their mark, whereas this man's hand probably hit out indiscriminately with the dull swipe of a bear's paw, and had driven Achim Uhland from this place long ago.

I started. Wasn't that a moped approaching? Quickly I retreated from the window and strained my ears to the darkness. I could hear nothing but the flickering drone of my own exhaustion, an internal noise that merged into the even background rhythms of the alley. Perhaps these had been interrupted by a particularly loud snore from the man behind the window, or by a particularly loud groan from the mill-wheel. The rain had soaked me to the skin under the torn, disintegrating material of my raincoat. A dark heat flowed through my head, spilling over and flooding my body with waves of icy shivers. Every breath ran onto a knife under my breastbone. The "houses", where I might have found somewhere dry, the attic perhaps, or at least the coal cellar, seemed like the other end of the earth. For a moment, I was on the point of ringing the door, but my brief determination to do so gave way to an involuntary whimper, and I sank into a heap on the doorstep. I knew I was finished. I had come to a dead end, and I felt an inexplicable sense of comfort in the thought that I might as well fall asleep on these steps, since Achim Uhland wouldn't be coming back here again anyway. I later discovered that my hunch hadn't been wrong. For him, too, a deceptive era of freedom had come to an end. He had broken into a jeweller's to steal a piece of jewellery for Manuela. He had beaten up the owner and was caught by the police while trying to get away. I was never to see him again.

There were suddenly torches flashing on me in the dark. The two policemen who had found me lying in the mud picked me up and dragged me to their car. I had finally succeeded in drawing the Germans' attention to myself. They asked me for my address and took me back to my father at the "houses".

How I managed to survive, and above all how you managed, I have no idea. But then perhaps you weren't the weaker one at all. Perhaps I owed my survival to you, to your stubborn will to live, forcing me to re-enter my body, forcing me to return from that twilight zone between life and death to the camp bed in my room which my father let me have as if he were granting a dog a corner in which to lie down and die. Perhaps you wrenched me back out of the darkness because you wanted to get to the light through me, and because you didn't know that you would have been much better off letting me die and dying inside me. You didn't realise that it would have been better for you to forestall me, because my survival meant a much crueller death for you than our dying together.

But we survived, you and I, inseparable as we were, and at last I noticed you, although you were already closer to your birth than to the act that engendered you. You came to my attention as something that made me feel part of human nature. That was probably the most astonishing thing about you! All of a sudden, I became aware of the simple fact of your existence in my body. You were the reason why I hadn't had a period for months, the reason for the strange vomiting which I had thought was an illness. And in the same moment I looked down and saw the clearly visible bulge of my belly. It all fitted together. Even with my vague knowledge of these things, I could see that one thing confirmed another, and from that moment I knew that you existed. And one of my first thoughts was that I must go and find the man who was your father. For a split second you gave me some sort of sense of belonging to him. For a split second I saw him as an ally, the person with whom I had you in common. And for that split second my only thought was to go and find him wherever he was, at the main station, or behind one of the windows that honeycombed the great grey streets, a man whose name I didn't know, a man who, thanks to you, really would have to marry me now and take me back to Persia – as a part of you. For a moment I was mad enough to think that you might help me find a home for myself, a family, a place of my own, and that through you I could become a human being, just as you wanted to become a human being through me. But behind this insane hope I already knew my situation was hopeless. For this hope was immediately followed by the certainty that only one of us would prevail. And in my knowledge that there was only one alternative, I was prepared to fight to the death. For we were enemies. We had always been enemies, locked in mortal combat. From the very first day, we had fought over the juice of every turnip I tore from the earth, over the goodness in every piece of bread I stole from my father, over every last calorie of warmth during the murderous nights of rain by the river. I hadn't realised that I had you to share with, a Moloch inside me, feeding on my unnourishing blood. I hadn't noticed your hunger inside me because my own was too great. I hadn't noticed your misery inside me because my own misery was normality, and I hadn't known that you were a part of my misery. And as if you'd known that I must be prevented from knowing this, you kept as quiet as you could inside me to the very last. Not once did I feel you move, as though the danger you were in forced you to play dead, just as I had played dead during the danger of the night you began.

Perhaps, like me, you knew that one movement could wake your murderer, and you crept away from me into the deepest, darkest corner you could find. Not once did you signal your presence to me. Perhaps you were simply too weak. But you couldn't hide from me for ever, not without arresting your own growth, not without dying of your own accord inside me. I had noticed you. I had located you inside me at last. And in so doing, I located him in me – your father.

But for a few days I loved you in spite of everything. You were the first person not to condemn me from the start, not to reject me out of hand, the first human being not to declare me nasty, dirty, inferior, wicked and guilty from the outset. You were the first person who hadn't already made up their mind about me. To you, I still had all of life before me; nothing had been ruled out, everything was open. You believed whatever I told you, even though I was sceptical myself, even though I did not believe in my own trustworthiness. I began to tell you this story even then, and you believed me. And although I thought of you merely as the punishment to fit my crime, as the shameful fruit of my original sin, manifest now to everybody else through you, you believed me, believed me even when I told you the very thing I believed least about myself – that I was not to blame for you. You saw a part of me I couldn't see. You saw me from inside, and you saw that I was good. I had chosen you of all people to see this, appointed you of all people to be my vindicator, my advocate, my guarantor, you of all people, who had more right than anyone else to mistrust me, since you were the object of my first ever decision to respond with destruction to something that was destroying me.

But for a few days I loved you and you returned my love. For a short time we were alone together in the world, you and I, mother and child, inseparable. And at last I was able to give to you what I had never experienced myself: security, affirmation, warmth and tenderness. I, who had never belonged anywhere, now belonged to you. You weren't a second, separate being who could leave me or reject me at any moment. You needed me, and for the first time in my life I meant something and had a value. I was not only no longer alone for the first time in my life; I was no longer a single being. And I now know that the only relief from the curse of womankind comes during this short period of not being one person – of being one flesh, one blood and one breath with another human being. This story is about the experience of extreme isolation, an elemental, human state of being, lived in its ultimate form by the homeless and by those who do not belong.

We had no future together, you and I. I was young. I was still a child myself, and I was still so ill and weak that I might not have survived your birth. I had no place to go to, let alone a place for you, let alone a place for us both. We had no future together. If you had been born, if you had survived, and if my father hadn't killed us both first, our only future would have been apart from one another, and your start in life would have been even blacker than my own. You would not only have been the continuation and repetition of me; you would have been an aggravated version of me. You would have been the nameless child of an unknown father, the child of an underage, social-misfit mother who didn't even own a rag to swaddle you in. You would not only have been the child of a Russian; you would have been a bastard of dubious skin colour, the mongrel offspring of two inferior races. To say nothing of the fact that you were also the child of someone who had been raped. That was the secret height of my own indecency and it would have been the worst of the blots on your life, too. It would have branded both of us; me as the one who had been raped, and you as the child of a rape, the fruit of an atrocity only inflicted upon those who deserve it. You were binding me to my destiny, a destiny it had been my sole purpose in life to escape, my sole desire, my sole guiding thought for as long as I could remember. My life, bound by this destiny, was worth nothing. It didn't interest me. I might just as well have thrown it away, crushed it beneath my foot, wiped it out. And you, a piece of flesh in my belly, had sealed this destiny. How was I to rip you out of me? You were the rapist in me. You were the duplicate of my father in me. Through you, I had become one flesh, one blood, one breath with everything I hated. And yet also through you, the man of whom you were a part had suddenly been delivered into my hands. I had him in my power. The wall of my abdomen was the only thing between me and him, between him and the knife I had lacked that night, the knife I had wanted to plunge into his sleeping body. He was still raping me. Every moment of your existence in me was rape, was the continuation of an expropriation that can only happen to a woman, can only be done to a woman by a man who rapes her and says to her by raping her: "I can penetrate you even without your consent. I can penetrate even to the most vulnerable, private part of your body. Even that belongs to me, and I shall do whatever I want with it." That is why soldiers in wartime violate the women of their enemies – in order to enact this ultimate form of expropriation. By raping the women they are conquering and subjugating the last piece of territory of the country they are humiliating and obliterating.

I couldn't save you any more than I had been saved myself. I was your Germany now, the Germany that had aborted me. You were now what I had once been in the hands of your fathers: a defenceless being at the mercy of someone who is stronger. I couldn't save you. My body had been your grave from the very beginning. The moment of your procreation was already the moment of your destruction.

I started by trying the same things everybody tried then. Those were the days of so-called shotgun weddings, and even I had heard of these methods. I jumped off the table dozens of times a day. I spent hours with my feet soaking in hot water. I didn't have the money to drink the prescribed gallons of Coca-Cola, but it occurred to me that I could use paraffin instead. We still had some in our cellar from the days before electric lights, and it once helped me kill the lice in my hair. With the aid of an enema, I pumped my stomach full of the stuff several times – in vain. I tried using various objects that were long and pointed and sharp – in vain. I tried all kinds of liquids and tools I found in the cellar and kitchen. Eventually, the first drops of bright red blood began to flow, the first drops of your life began to pass from me. I spent that night in pain, the worst pain I had ever known. Your death struggle had begun inside me, and it looked for a while as if you were going to survive the night victorious, as if we were going to remain inseparable for ever. I had only managed to tear a part of you out of me: your head, and your arms which I had pulled on to rip you out of me. A part of you, the part that contained your heart, floated away in the sewers that night, floated away behind my emerald-green eyes which the mirror above the wash-basin recorded for all time in that night of blood. A part of you was floating in the sewers, while the rest of you held fast until morning, held onto me like a tenacious root, like claws dug into my flesh. I fought what was left of you, your dead remains that refused to release me, determined to take me with you into the subterranean town as though we were an indivisible whole. But in the end you did let me go. You gave me my life. Unlike you, I had survived this ordeal, too. And shortly afterwards, all my dreams came true. I got my German husband and my German house. I became engaged and had a white wedding. I became the wife of the most German man there was. I married a German neo-Nazi who was ten years older than me, the son of a former Nazi *gauleiter*. And everything I have told you in this story was nothing compared to the moment of awakening that was to follow this marriage, the first moment of light to enter this story of darkness.

My father, your father, our father, died a quarter of a century later, long after this darkness. He died during the course of my soliloquy with you. I watched him follow you. I had seen the cobalt blue eyes of an embryo opened wide in astonishment, poised before the black floodgate of life. And I saw him pass through this floodgate in the opposite direction. It is no longer my business to forgive him, but yours.

I am taking my leave of you, my child. You never became a child, and I have never become a mother. The chain was broken. There is no one to follow me. No sister of yours, no brother. There is no one to continue this story. The life my parents brought with them to Germany will die out with me.

And yet what a pity it is that you will never know this life! You will never know immortality holding onto your mother's hand. You will never witness this day with the gorse in front of my window blossoming against death and hell on earth. You will never hear the stillness I hear now. You will never be able to say as I have said: "Once I lived like the gods, and more we do not need . . ."

Founded in 1986, Serpent's Tail publishes the innovative and the challenging.

If you would like to receive a catalogue of our current publications please write to:

FREEPOST
Serpent's Tail
4 Blackstock Mews
LONDON N4 2BR

(No stamp necessary if your letter is posted in the United Kingdom.)